650

W9-BLK-662

*Jodi Barrows*
*2011*

My wish is for you to be encouraged by
these women, inspired to create the quilts,
and motivated to live life to the fullest.
Stay focused on the dash of your gravestone.
It represents your life.

~ Jodi Barrows

*Editor:* Jodi Barrows, Tucker Barrows, Linda Watts

*Additional editing:* Jenny Singleton, Martha Fitts

# Our Family Line

Moses Gimlin    Austin Gimlin
7.22.1858        8.14.1818

Harris/Tate
Married 6.5.1898

Pa & Granny
Gimlin

Izell Gimlin

Mineola Tate

Izell                    Lillie
Mineola Tate Thomas

# 5 Generations of Women

# Dedication

This book is dedicated to the women that came before me: my mother Elwanda Irwin, grandmother Izelle Gimlin, great-grandmother Mineola Thomas, and my great Aunt Lillie Morrison. Their strength, courage and perseverance continue to influence my life.

# *Mailly Family Tree*

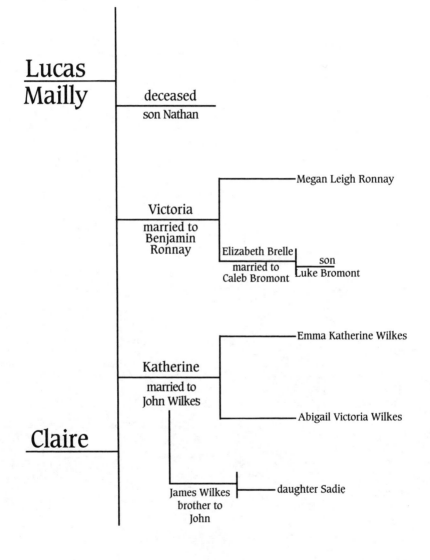

Lucas
Mailly

deceased
son Nathan

Victoria
married to
Benjamin
Ronnay

Megan Leigh Ronnay

Elizabeth Brelle
married to
Caleb Bromont

son
Luke Bromont

Katherine
married to
John Wilkes

Emma Katherine Wilkes

Abigail Victoria Wilkes

Claire

James Wilkes
brother to
John

daughter Sadie

x

# Introduction

As I was growing up in my family, I heard many stories from my mother, aunts and grandmothers. All of these women have lived to be ninety plus in years and kept their mind sharp. They even lived in their own homes and cared for themselves up to their death. All were widowed at a young age and never remarried. They had remarkable lives and I always gained strength and courage from their experiences.

My ancestors were very much "a lady" respecting etiquette and fine manners. They didn't hesitate to do what needed to be done without any male help or influence.

Many of the situations that you will read about in my story are real. It really happened to someone in my family tree.

I was taught to sew by my mother and grandmother. It just seemed natural to mix in the heavy quilting theme.

The Mailly family will extend for one hundred and fifty years or more. The next novel, will pick up right where this one pauses.

I hope you enjoy the quilts and the women who created them.

You may go to the Leaving Riverton website for more information, sample chapters and to see the quilts. www.LeavingRiverton.com. Send me an e-mail. I would love to hear from you. snsjodi@yahoo.com.

# Chapter 1
## A Spring Night

### 1856 - Central Louisiana

THE APRILS IN LECOMPTE are spectacular months. At the
beginning of them, the trees are bare from winter and look
unpromising, but by the third week they burst with new life
and become green all over again. They transform from skinny trees to
fat trees, all in a few days. It is quite hot though during this month, and
muggy-humid. The days are long and lingering, but when night comes
the air is less thick and becomes more pleasant-which makes for
excellent evenings outside with family.

The trees were still budding with the colors of spring when
Elizabeth stepped out onto the wooden porch that surrounded her
home. From the steps, far-flung strikes of lightning collided with night
clouds. In the distance, a nearly full moon hung brilliantly over the

ageless oak trees that bordered the river and the house. A raccoon clicked his forest call; an unexpected wind ruffled leaves and called out goose bumps.

"Oh how I love this place," she thought.

She loved the white porch that overlooked the river, the barn, and the timber mill that her grandfather owned. She loved the house, with its pointy, gabled roof that it wore like a carefully knitted hat. She loved everything about Lecompte, and didn't want to leave anything of it at all behind.

Her family had lived in Louisiana for close to ninety-five years. She often wondered if she had the courage to leave it all, and start a new life someplace else, far from here.

She took a long breath, almost to become closer to her surroundings. She wanted her home to seep even deeper into her heart. She wouldn't allow herself to forget anything of it. A single tear slid down her cheek and stopped under her chin, like a raindrop on the brink of falling from a rooftop, it stayed there.

Her great-grandfather settled on this very piece of land that had been home for four generations. He brought his bride here. Her Grandpa Lucas was born in this very house. He raised his two daughters on this riverbank, both of whom married southern gentlemen and later moved away.

Elizabeth's parents had died when she was only six and her sister Megan was just two. Their untimely death had shocked the family. So Elizabeth and Megan were brought to live with their Grandpa Lucas, who owned the Riverton Timber Mill.

She scanned the night sky again as new raindrops hopped around on the steps and then ran together and formed a puddle around the magnolia tree. Her Grandpa Lucas had always said that the river made this place ageless; it was renewed everyday. The water moved as it brought new life and swept away the old. She had to memorize every part of it. She reached out and touched the thick, waxy leaves of the magnolia tree that lived just outside her window. Its blooms were round like tea saucers and nearly the size of dinner plates, in full budding mode. Their calming smell radiated over the porch and filled the night air.

"How could I leave this house, the only home I've ever known?"

The moon looked out and showed his face behind passing clouds as Elizabeth sat brooding at the night sky.

# Chapter 2
## Like Only Sisters Can

ELIABETH WAS SITTING across from her Grandpa Lucas in the comfortable parlor that had always been home. Gardenias, from her garden, floated through the open window and filled the room with their sweet scent. The curtains hung on a recent breeze from outside.

With a smile that reflected the wisdom of many years, he took her hand and patted it with his work-worn hands. "Liz," he said. "This will be dangerous, you know that. But it's the only choice we have now." Grandpa Lucas looked up at Liz. She was silent.

"I only wish there was another way, but there isn't," he said.

"So do I."

"In two weeks, we will have to leave here."

Grandpa Lucas stood up and faced the fireplace, his back to her. His hand went up to his face quickly and then to the faded photo that lived on the mantel. His face turned away from her. Liz could see that he was wiping away an unwelcome tear that he didn't want her to notice. She blinked back a tear of her own and took a quick breath to steady her emotions. She knew that her grandfather was troubled at the idea of sending his granddaughters to Texas alone, unaided and unaccompanied.

"I got another letter from Abby and Emma. It arrived yesterday," she said cheerfully, trying to break the silence. "They are excited about the trip, but it seems that there is some sort of holdup with Sadie."

"With Sadie," he asked curiously.

"Yes. Exactly what, I don't know."

"You hardly know her. How will . . ."

"I know Grandpa, but you must admit that another woman to go along would be nice."

"Liz, you don't realize. Not all women are as strong as you and your sister. They will only hold you back."

"Grandpa, it will be fine; but I don't want for you to worry about it," she said, trying to appear modest. She had grown accustomed to his constant praises. He was quite proud of his granddaughters and his great-grandson Luke. They were all he had.

"I just don't like the idea," he paused. "Liz, you've been through a great deal these last few months, but you're stronger now. I can see it. But know this, Luke is growing up and will be a man soon. Let him grow up and become a man."

Liz didn't say anything, not because she didn't agree, but because she did, and she knew he was right.

"Caleb would have been proud of you," he said.

Liz suddenly felt like crying.

With a sense of urgency, she stood up and brushed her skirt out. She wouldn't let her emotions get to her. Losing her husband, Caleb, in a timber accident had been almost too much for her. It had happened at the mill almost eleven months ago. It had all seemed like a horrible nightmare that she was unable to wake from, and since then, the accident seemed to linger like fog in her mind.

Grandpa Lucas was afraid that he would never get his lovely granddaughter back after the accident. He and his grandson, his namesake, had grown even closer as Liz drifted away, just as her husband had, rolling obliviously under the logs and frothy water. For Liz, the only way to continue was to stay busy and keep moving forward. This kept her mind from drifting away to the sadness of losing a husband. The sadness was like a husband-shaped hole in her heart that could never again be mended or filled. She wanted a new beginning.

In fact, a new beginning was what the whole family desired. They wanted someplace different, where deep-rooted memories could be forgotten and new ones made. Adding to this, the tremors of war seemed to be shaking stronger and more determined within the community-which made Grandpa Lucas even antsier to get going with his plan of leaving.

The idea of going west gave Elizabeth a feeling of adventure that she loved. It would keep her mind where it needed to be, in the future and far from the past. Since Liz was the oldest and most able, she would be in charge of her little band of women, looking for a new life.

"Grandpa, I think it would be best if Luke stays here with you."

"For the trip you mean?"

"Yes."

Grandpa Lucas rubbed his chin. "And join later?"

"Yes."

"I don't understand. Why do you want for him to stay?"

"I think that it would be best for him."

"Liz, it could be seven months before I even leave for Texas. I just can't leave before the mill and property are sold."

"I know Grandpa. Somehow, I just think you should stay together.

I don't want anything to happen to either of you." She could feel the tears swelling up behind her eyelids. She blinked again to fight them from coming. She felt like such a crier.

Where was that strong, levelheaded girl that Grandpa had always loved and admired? Will I ever be that person again?
Grandpa Lucas swayed back and forth from left foot to right foot, but didn't say anything.

"Luke misses his dad," Liz declared. "He needs to be around another man."

"I suppose I should think about this…"

"And if Caleb is still alive somewhere, and finds his way home, Luke will be here!" She immediately felt silly for holding on to the idea that her husband was still alive, but it just seemed like something inside of her, some sort of innate whim that she couldn't quite let go of yet. Her mind clung to the idea that he was just away for a while and that he would be back. She liked it better, so she could keep going. But lately, it seemed like there were two sides to her, and she could sense this. Sometimes she felt she could move on, maybe even find a husband; other times, she wasn't sure.

Grandpa Lucas paused, preparing Elizabeth for his words. "Liz, you have to come to terms with this…Caleb is gone. He's not coming back." He stepped closer to hug her. His broad shoulders and loving blue eyes embraced her tightly. "You know its been long enough for him to have been found. You have to move forward with your life now. It's not going to get any better here. War will develop in these states." Elizabeth hugged her grandfather and cried into his chest. Her tears left little damp stains on his shirt. She looked up at him and kissed his cheek.

"I made your shirt wet," she said.

"It's no matter," he chuckled, pulling his shirt out to have a better look at it.

They both looked at his shirt and laughed. It had actually become quite wet from her tears. You could see the faint impression from where her eyes and mouth were two sockets and an oval. It looked like a large dairy cow had been crying on his shirt.

Elizabeth knew that her grandfather was right though, and that it would be best if they continued on with their plan to sell the timber mill in return for gold. She knew that, according to her grandfather, gold would be the most stable form of currency if war did erupt. Something that at this point, seemed rather likely.

Grandpa Lucas' eyes followed Liz as she walked quickly to the parlor doorway. Luke was standing outside the door, straight like an arrow, his messy sun-streaked hair over his eyes. He looked exactly like his father. Liz would never forget the face of her Caleb, for she only had to look at her son to remember. The latter was now standing before both of them and staring with eyes that seemed to shoot fire. He stepped closer to his great-grandfather and mother.

"That cannot happen Grandpa! Tell me you will not allow it."
Liz searched her mind for the part that Luke had overheard. "What can't happen?" she thought.

"I must go; you must allow me to go with you!"

"Darling." Liz reached out her arms to her son. Grandpa Lucas put out his arm to stop her.

"Let him be a man," she remembered.
Liz felt snubbed.

Grandpa Lucas turned to his grandson. "Luke, you mustn't be so concerned about this. We know what is best for you."

"I cannot stay here grandfather. I want to go along."

"I know that you do darling," Liz said, "but Grandpa and I must consider this."

"But you said it was settled already, that I could go." He looked over to Liz. "If you don't allow me, then I'll join th'...the Union Army." He blurted out like an afterthought.

Liz looked stunned.

"With those Yankees?" Liz said, mostly to herself.

"Luke, your mother and I will consider this, but you will not join the war regardless of what is decided."

"Grandfather, I would not want to join the war. I only don't want to be left here."

"I know Luke, but don't be anxious. I know what is best for you."

"I know." Lucas murmured.

"Settle it with your mother now and give her a kiss. We need to finish the fence. I've spent too much time on it already. We must finish the posts today. It has taken us far too long."

Young Luke felt satisfied with his grandfather's news. In the past, "thinking about it" had normally tilted in his favor. He wiped his eyes and looked at his grandfather. He hated crying in front of them. He didn't want to be treated as a "darling," but he knew that he was the only one that could change the tune of that whistle.

Luke kissed his mother on the cheek and then walked out of the parlor with his great-grandfather at his side-still a full head shorter than him, but trying to catch up.

"Will we still go fishing, Grandpa?"

"Yes, but first the fence. It will not take us much time at all."
Liz watched them disappear through the front door. She walked deeper into the parlor, sinking herself into the comfy chair that was situated by the window. She was barely over the accustomed mourning period and did not yet have the strength for life. She sat there, on the verge of sleep.

She thought of her patch of flowers that she had recently planted and looked out to make sure they were still alive. "They need more water again," she thought. "Or they'll dry up and die."

The sweet smell of her garden flowers seeped into the room and filled it like tea from a teabag. She took a deep breath and looked across the room to Caleb's green quilt. The only thing that would get her out of bed during that time of mourning was to work on her husband's quilt. She closed her eyes in exhaustion. Her mind began to wander.

She remembered that it was a gray and cloudy day in May of 1855. The clouds swirled in the air; the rain was soaking and surprisingly cold. It was the sort of day in the life of a family where something feels bound to happen that could split it apart.

"The air doesn't feel right, the rain is too wet."

It was the sort of day where something happens to prod life's brittleness from its sleeping place and make it crawl to the surface and roar for a while, out in the open.

Liz was sitting in the parlor working on her most recent quilting project. She had named it Caleb's Choice. She was quilting it when a winded Luke came crashing into the house, calling "Mom, mom come quick!"

"What is it?"

"It's dad. He's fallen into the logs…!"

The ground was saturated with rain and the grass looked limp and lifeless as she rushed to the mill. Her mind raced. The wind blew fiercely. Trees bent. Leaves clung. Liz ran through mud, and the rain shattered against her face and eyes. She couldn't feel the rain's wetness or its cold sting. Her mind opened and the thoughts and possibilities poured in like the intense rain against her face.

"A horse to slide, a dock to fall," as she approached the mill and waterway.

As always, they were behind on the timber orders. Grandpa Lucas and Caleb worked long and hard everyday, never demanding more from their workers than they themselves were willing to give.

"It's their fault, it's everybody's fault!"

Rain soaked and muddy, she stood there with hair pressed to her head. She watched the mill workers standing in silence with faces completely baffled and afraid.

"He's gone Liz. We couldn't reach him," Grandpa Lucas confessed.

"I'm sorry Liz, I couldn't get to him in time," Thomas said in tears.

Their words shot through her like a heavy, steel pistol. She looked away and fell to the ground.

Nobody had told her how long it was before she woke up in her own bed. Maybe days had passed. She remembered that when she awoke that day the sun was out and the property was dry, the grass had changed an immodest green. Her son was asleep across the end of the bed. Her sister Megan sat in a chair that hugged tightly against the side of the bed, threading a needle with embroidery floss.

*...clip clop, clop clop...*

The clopping of horses jolted Liz awake, her hands shaking and sweaty. She looked outside the parlor window to see the clop and clatter of horse hooves as they approached the house. Someone from the mill was unloading wooden crates and old cloths to use for packing.

Across, on the other side of the parlor, Caleb's quilt laid over the back of a small chair, now completed. She walked over to it and brought it close to her face, running her hand over the sewn patches of tans, reds, and greens.

"Caleb would have loved it," she thought.

She had made it for their thirteenth wedding anniversary. Luke was now twelve and she would be thirty-two by summer. She had been a widow for almost a full year. Most of the time, she felt that she could never love again, but other times, she thought that she might be able to, if, of course, she was introduced to the right man. Several southern gentlemen had made their courting desires known to Grandpa Lucas. He had even tried to convince her to see Doc Gaither. He was handsome and agreeable, but Liz loved Caleb. She missed his smile, the two freckles on his ear, but mostly she had missed watching him be a father to Luke.

Across the hall, the bustle and stir of Megan's treadle machine brought Liz to the doorway where she stood. Megan sat sewing pieces on her new treadle. She was slightly shorter than average, some might even call her petite, with dark, straight hair that had an attractive shine to it. Her eyes were a hazy green, big, and intent; their gaze suggested that she was passionate, but playful and happy. She peddled hard, her shoulders even with the movement of the machine with her hair swaying this way and that.

The quilt top that she was working on was a cream-red and blue. It was almost complete, but it would be dark soon and she would have to light the lamp for the evening. Liz didn't like it when she worked by lamp-light. There was so much shifting and motion that Liz was afraid of the lamp falling and causing a fire. Liz had always been protective of her sister.

Megan slowed the motion of the treadle wheel and looked up.

"I think that Luke will probably go with us when we leave for Texas next week," Liz said.

"What happened? I thought that you were against it," Megan asked.

"I told him that Grandpa and I would consider it; but now that I think of it, we could use him."

"Yes, we certainly could."

"I suppose so."

"I've thought so all along, really."

"Yes?"

"There are many things that we could use him for," Megan assured her, pausing briefly. "What happened?"

"Well, Luke overheard Grandpa and I discussing the trip and suggested that he would join the Union Army if he were forbade to come."

"The war that doesn't yet exist?"

"Yes!" Liz said laughing. "Grandpa has convinced him."

They both giggled at Luke's idea.

"I know that it is safer for him here Liz, but I think we could use him a lot more if he were to go with us. He can even go to school there."

"Yes, I had thought of it as well."

"Oh Liz! I didn't tell you. I got a letter today from Pastor Parker and his wife."

"You did? I must've been sleeping. Did you read it yet?"

"Yes, I did. And well, by fall, they will have the church prepared for holding class, and they want Abby to teach there!"

"Oh Meggie, that's wonderful."

"Yes, in an extra room they are preparing. I can't wait to tell her."

"She will be delighted. When will they be here?"

"On Thursday, their stage should arrive late afternoon."

"I must say Meggie, I'm growing rather excited about our journey."

"Me too, I am very excited."

"I wonder if Abby and Emma are as excited?"

"Oh, they must be!"

Liz and Megan heard the jangling of the wagon as it rolled away from the house, the dust trailing just behind. She must have slept for a longer time than she realized-through post diggings and fence mendings-because Grandpa Lucas and Luke were already leaving to fish. She watched their lanterns dangle from the side posts of the wagon, which they would use to fish with once it got dark. They had always fished at night because Grandpa Lucas said that it was best to fish then; that's when the most fish were caught he said, and they believed him.

"Where are the Lukes off to?" Megan asked.

"Grandpa wanted to take Luke for one final fishing trip."

"Oh, maybe we'll have catfish for supper."

"Yes, it's never certain though when those two go fishing," Liz laughed. "When was the last time they caught something?"

Liz and Megan both laughed. They had always joked about the Lukes' fishing trips, but mostly about whether or not there were any fish at all to be caught in that pond.

"Oh, is that Granny's pattern?" Liz asked.

They both gazed at the cotton top. It was a lovely pieced appliqué with nine beautiful flower blocks. The triangles were various, and meticulously pieced together so that the corners ran smooth and flat against the borders. The pattern was a simple garden design and very beautiful.

Liz traced her fingers over the seams and down its edges.

"Yes, it is. It has ended up gorgeous. Don't you think?"

"Of course, it's beautiful! I simply adore this pattern. Do you remember the one she made with the pastel fabrics and the paisley border? She always loved appliqué, as do I."

"Yes, I do. It was very pretty."

"You've finished so quickly Meggie. It looks wonderful, though."

"Thank you," Megan glowed. "I would like to have this one in its frame by morning."

"Oh! Well, I can't wait to see it. I can help if you'd like."

"Fine. I imagine that Abby and Emma will want to help as well."

"Lovely then!"

They stood in silence for a moment. Megan hovered over the treadle and concentrated on the needle in her hand. Liz was looking out the window at the red barn.

"Liz, have you been to the mill to speak with Thomas yet?"

"What do you mean?" Liz asked naively. "For what reason would I have to speak with him?"

"I think that you should speak with him Liz. Especially before we leave."

"What are you talking about Meggie? What do I have to speak with him about?"

"Lizzie, he loves you. How can you not know this?"

"What do you mean he loves me?"

"He's loved you even before you were a widow. He's always loved you."

"How do you...?" Liz's face flushed red. "Why would he feel that way?"

"Liz, you can't help who you love. It just happens."

"How could I do that to Caleb? I just couldn't."

"Do you not think that Caleb would want you to be happy, Lizzie?"

"It's without purpose. We are leaving in a few days."

"Well, yes!" Megan shouted, as though stumbling upon something. "You should at least show an interest is all. You will never know what might happen."

"I don't know. It's too soon Megan. Once you've loved someone then you will understand. How can you know about love?"

"So you're just going to be a widow for the rest of your life?"

Megan's words were cutting, even though they weren't intended to be. Like a skilled farmer with a sickle, family always knew where it was best to cut. They knew your fears, which at times gave them an uneven advantage. Liz was afraid. Being a widow for the rest of her life was something that had always frightened her. She didn't want to end up that way.

"Oh Liz, I'm sorry. Don't cry, Lizzie. Please don't cry," Megan said, wrapping her arms around her sister. "I didn't mean for you to cry." She had never before seen her cry like this, so powerfully. Megan immediately felt horrible for it. Even months before, at Caleb's memorial, she had not cried like this.

She held her sister tighter, as though it would make it better the closer she held her. For a moment, she felt a glimpse of what it was like to be an older sister, caring for Liz like she had always been cared for as a child.

They stood there, next to the treadle, saying nothing, but loving each other like only sisters can.

# Chapter 3
## *Black Currant Tea*

L IZ PLACED CALEB'S QUILT at the foot of her bed, it dipped down and touched the wooden floor. She smoothed it with her hand, fixing the wrinkles she had made from sleeping the night before. She glanced at the empty side of the bed.

Yesterday, and all of this morning, Liz had contemplated what Megan had suggested the afternoon before about Thomas.

"Perhaps, I should speak with him," Liz thought.

The sound of horses, from outside, brought Liz and Megan to the front porch. They looked out over the railing. It was now late in the afternoon and quite muggy from the night's rain. Springtime in Louisiana had always been a hot, mulling spell. The daytime air was damp and heavy-like moss that hangs and gathers on trees by a river's edge.

Today, however, seemed especially humid. She ran her hand across the back of her neck. The back of her dress stuck to her shoulders. Eight wooden wagons met in the yard and in front of the barn. The mill workers were unloading empty crates and boxes of sawdust from the mill.

"Miss Elizabeth. Miss Megan. Good afternoon," Thomas said in full stride as he approached the steps.

"Good afternoon," they said politely.

"We're unloading these crates," Thomas said.

"Oh good, the crates," Megan said, inspecting them from a distance.

"Yes, we also brought the sawdust to pack your breakables and things for the trip."

"Wonderful," Liz said.

"It was just as easy to bring the wagons too." He paused, looking over at the wagons. "There they are."

Everyone looked over at the wagons rowed up in the yard.

"When will more of the horses arrive?" Megan asked.

"In a few days. Yes, probably Monday."

Megan could see Grandpa Lucas motioning for her from the side of the wagon. She gave a polite gesture to Thomas and hastily walked down the stairs to meet him. Grandpa Lucas had a mischievous look on his face that she wasn't use to seeing. They both exchanged whispers and looked conspicuously over to the couple standing in silence under the porch.

Grandpa Lucas had wanted nothing more than for Liz to be happy, and he was quite partial to Thomas. He knew how Liz felt. Over twenty years ago, his wife Claire and son had died, and he never remarried. It was different for a man though, he had the mill and the farm and the two granddaughters to look after. His Claire could never be replaced. Although, he never really did look. Not too long ago, however, Liz and Megan had told him about a widow his age that lived just outside of town. She had made it known that she was interested in him, but he was insulted by the thought of it; and afterwards, he had stopped going to any of the church socials.

"Thomas," Liz said, all of a sudden feeling uncomfortable standing next to him alone, "I suppose that I should let you know something," she said pensively.

Thomas was surprised at her. Liz too was surprised at herself. It had just slipped out.

Thomas focused his gaze and listened anxiously. His silent attention somehow made her uneasy though, and she quickly lost her words.

"Ohm," she mumbled.

He sensed her nervousness; he moved closer, thinking this would calm her.

Liz all of a sudden was afraid that he would try to place his hand on her arm; she took a small step backwards to avoid him. Her foot searched for a step behind her. A wood board creaked under the weight of her foot and startled her. She tried to adjust her footing, but her balance shifted on the top step. Somehow, she had lost control of her feet. Her hands and arms rummaged desperately for a post, a column, a something; but she couldn't find anything.

"I'm going to fall," dashed through her mind.

And flat on her fanny she fell.

As she hit the ground, a burst of laughter erupted from the yard. Everyone had seen the whole thing; the whole embarrassing ordeal. She looked up to Thomas and the mill workers and everyone laughing at her. All she could do was laugh at herself; she was sick of crying.

"Nothing to see here, nothing to see," Thomas said, waving his arms at everyone and trying to be funny.

"Ahh, are you all right?" Grandpa Lucas asked with hand extended.

"Yes, yes. I'm fine. I don't know what is wrong with me."

"Lizzie," Megan teased. "Did someone move the porch?"

Another small burst of laughter erupted among the bystanders. Liz smiled and tried to act busy dusting the ground off her dress. She had needed a good laugh.

The mill workers were pleased with the disturbance that had interrupted work, and now walked back to the wagons with smiles and recaps of the incident with a "Didyousee," and an "Andthenshe." They laughed.

"Are you okay," Thomas asked now with everyone gone.

"Yes, I'm fine."

"Good, I didn't mean to cause that…if I did."

"Would you like some currant tea?" Liz asked.

"Please, I'm quite thirsty."

"Okay, I will bring it to you on the porch then."

Liz quickly disappeared into the kitchen.

THE FRONT YARD WAS now bustling again with mill workers and wagons and unloading, preparing to leave for the day. Liz and Thomas sat on the porch sipping currant tea, and somehow pleased by being separated from it all. They felt mischievous for it, like they should be working but weren't. They would help later, they agreed.

Luke was hunched over the porch steps with the catfish fillets he had recently caught. They waited to be breaded and cooked. Barn cats hovered about, waiting for their chance to have a taste.

"Would you like to stay for dinner?" Liz inquired. "We're having catfish."

"Yes, all right. Catfish sounds delicious."

"Great then, I think Grandpa would like to discuss some things of the trip with you."

Liz gathered her thoughts, preparing to change the subject.

"I want you to know that I've really appreciated all that you've done for us, for Luke and the mill and everything."

"Yes, I've enjoyed working for your grandfather. He's a good man."

"Yes, he's a great man. I love him dearly."

Thomas nodded in agreement.

Liz hands were wrapped tightly around her tea glass. "I am going to put the marker on the hill for Caleb in the morning, and I would like for you to come with me."

"Yes, that's what I…"

"Liiiiizie," Megan interrupted from inside as she stepped out onto the porch. "Oh, sorry! I didn't know you were out here Thomas," she said with cornmeal on her hands. "Well, dinner will be ready soon. But could you give me a hand, Liz? I need your help with *something*," she winked.

"Yes, I'll be right in."

"Thomas, are you staying for dinner," Grandpa Lucas said merrily as he approached the front steps.

Liz intervened, "Yes, he is."

"Good then, we've got so much catfish that we could never eat it all."

"Mom, is Thomas staying for dinner tonight?" Luke asked excitedly.

"Yes, honey; he's staying for dinner."

"Well…uh, after dinner Thomas, we could whittle some if you would like."

"Fine, we could make something for your mother and aunt. Maybe a spool or something."

"Dear," Liz said. "Let's come inside and see if Megan needs our help with anything."

He walked into the house with Liz straggling just behind. Thomas and Grandpa Lucas loitered on the front porch, looking out at the dusky sky, at nothing in particular. It was close to evening now, the sun dipped down below the trees, not quite ready to set just yet, but preparing to. The locusts were already out, singing their low croak from tree to tree. The sky was a pale blue with magnificent pinks, reds, and oranges showing themselves through clouds and final beams of sunlight.

"What an incredible sunset," Grandpa Lucas suggested while chewing the stem of his tobacco-less pipe. He had no tobacco because the general store happened to be out of his brand, and he hated Lyon tobaccos.

"It is especially incredible tonight. Isn't it?"

"Mmm hm," Grandpa Lucas said, in some form of masculine agreement.

A long silence came over the porch and filled the air, but this was quite normal for men. It was even expected while standing on the porch with them. They were just more comfortable with the idea of silence. It wasn't at all awkward.

"Well," Grandpa Lucas said, breaking the silence. "I have been thinking some and I must say that I don't feel completely at ease with sending my granddaughters alone on this trip. I just don't like the idea." He paused for a moment. "I have made plans for them to have an escort for part of the way, with the Rangers from Texas, but I am still not eased by this."

"I can understand that. I think it's normal, sir."

"The reason I'm telling you this, Thomas is because I would like for you to go along with them and be their escort."

Thomas paused for a moment, thinking about what to say. "And this would make you at ease if I were to go along with them?" Grandpa Lucas chuckled and pulled out his pipe to examine it. He had a humorous, jolly laugh, just as you might expect him to have for a man of his size. And when he laughed, he made others laugh. His laugh was especially contagious, like all laughter tends to be.

Thomas couldn't help but laugh too. Though, he wasn't sure what about.

"Thomas, I don't think anything would ease my mind completely, but it would make me more at ease."

"I see."

"But I also know that the ladies and Luke too, would want more for you to go than any of the other mill workers."

"Really?"

"Yes," Grandpa Lucas assured him. "So what will you say? You can think about it some if you'd like…"

"I'll do it then sir," Thomas blurted out with excitement. He offered his hand to Lucas and they shook hands fiercely.

"Dinner is ready!" Megan called from the door.

"Great, I'm starved." Grandpa Lucas said with his hand around the back of Thomas' shoulder. "Let's go eat. We can discuss the details later."

# Chapter 4
## Caleb's Hill

THE NEXT MORNING WAS SO DIM AND FOGGY that dawn had the hardest time breaking. Liz could barely see the corner of the barn from the house; its red outline poking out through the muddled mistiness. The fog had a way of filtering out any distant noises until they were near. So when Thomas' carriage showed up in the yard, it was actually the sudden jolt of the horse that made her aware of his arrival.

Thomas wore his wool hat and boots, which seemed rather odd to Liz considering that it was April. She quickly forgot about this soon after he arrived. The large wooden marker and two shovels laid in the wagon, and about ten feet of rope. Liz wasn't sure what the rope was for, but she didn't ask either way.

"Good morning!" Thomas called from the wagon, stepping down.

"How are you?"

"Good morning. I'm fine, a little tired, however," Liz said cheerfully.

"Yes, me too." Thomas said, brushing something from the horse. "Can you believe this fog?"

"Yes, I know. It's quite thick isn't it," she said, looking around as though she might peer through it. "Won't you be unable to see?"

"Let's hope not," he grinned.

Liz smiled and laughed.

"Well, shall we?"

Thomas helped Liz up into the wagon and they were on their way. From the house, it looked as though they had disappeared into the heavy morning. Megan was watching from the kitchen doorway with a smile. She was happy for her sister. Happy that she was finally closer to understanding the passing of her husband; and that, perhaps, after eleven months, she could now move on.

It wasn't too far to the hill, where the family gravesite was kept. On the way, the little lives that lived only at night were scurrying around, not yet aware that it was morning and the sun would be bright soon. A dull green bullfrog waited in a scummy waterhole, desperately hoping to catch some breakfast before it was too bright and his cover blown. As they moved up the hill, normally, all of their world could be seen; today however, the fog was too thick. On a clear day, the mill could be seen next to the river-which was also the first thing one could see when traveling along the main road. On the slope behind it were the small cabins where some of the mill workers stayed. Most, however, lived in Lecompte or Meeker, which were just a few minutes from the mill. Farther up the path, and closer to the house, was the barn and stable where the horses and chickens lived; and, of course, Belle, the very old cow that had outlived two coats of milk paint on the barn.

Once there, Thomas jumped down and immediately helped Elizabeth from her seat in the wagon. He then grabbed the larger shovel and began digging a hole to place the marker. Liz watched from the side of the wagon, trying to sit and balance herself on the wooden wheel. She quickly gave up and decided to help with the digging.

After a few minutes the hole was deep enough. Thomas carried the wooden marker from the back of the wagon to the grassy area, inspecting the paint along the way. He had made it at Liz's request almost two weeks ago. It was a large white cross, made of pine and painted carefully all the way around. Thomas had also made a square marker for its base and written across it:

> *To a friend who gave us all the friendship,*
> *We will miss you.*
> *To a father who fathered honorably,*
> *You won't be forgotten*
> *To a husband who loved faithfully,*
> *Your memory will never fade from our hearts.*

Thomas placed the memorial in its hole and carefully packed dirt all the way around its base. He then secured the square marker to the bottom of the cross and stood back to examine his work.

He felt obligated to say something, so he decided to recite the words from the epitaph that he had painted on the marker. Afterwards, it was silent again. Liz didn't say anything.

They both stood there, around the newly placed marker, each remembering Caleb in their own way.

After a long period of stillness, Elizabeth walked over to pickup her shovel and placed it in the back of the wagon. Across, on the other side, Thomas still knelt beside the marker, remembering his close friend whom he had known since childhood. He was crying.

Caleb's death hadn't just been difficult for Liz and Luke; the whole town had been affected. He was a well-known and well-liked person of the town, and over two hundred people were at his memorial service.

The entire town population had been there, even some people from Pineville showed up. But after eleven months, Liz pushed herself to move forward, and now she felt that she was most apt to do so. She knew that Thomas still held a heavy burden for Caleb's death. In a way, he almost felt responsible for it.

"Thank you Thomas," Liz said, "for everything you've done. I could never tell you how grateful I am, really."

Thomas had become rather emotional and wasn't able to say anything, but it didn't really seem that he needed to say anything. Liz knew that he had risked his life going in after Caleb, and she felt that she could never repay him for it. She felt so indebted to him, considering that he was willing to give his life in order to save her husband.

After a moment, Thomas stood up and placed his shovel in the rear of the wagon.

They slowly loaded up again and were on their way, both glancing at the memorial as they rode past. Neither of them had realized it, but the fog had cleared up almost completely. The sun was now out and shining brightly; and there wasn't a single cloud to be found in the sky.

# Chapter 5
## The Wilke Sisters

ABBY AND EMMA WERE TIRED from their extended journey from Mississippi, the western part, close to the Great River. It had taken them five days. One day to travel from Charleston to the river docks, by stagecoach, of course. After that, two days to ride a riverboat down the Mississippi, stopping only once along the way; and finally, another two days to travel into Lecompte.

The stagecoach bounced recklessly along the rocky path. The luggage on top made tumbling-off noises, as it had for two days now. Emma looked back, nothing had fallen.

Emma had loved watching the riverboats that traveled along the Mississippi. They were large and churning, their stately red paddle fins rising with dignity over the dark waters. They made stirring noises in the water, which were oddly reassuring to passengers, almost calming. The ride was pleasant though, not like two days on a rattling stage. The waters were smooth, slightly rippled looking, like stained glass in a church. Viny trees looked out and hung over, and watched boats as they churned past. Slowly. Proudly.

They waited anxiously now for the edge of the small town to appear in view. It had been almost nine years since they had seen their cousins and the Mailly family. Over the years though, they had exchanged letters and packages of wildflower seeds; and, of course, the occasional, or even quite frequent, pouches of fabric scraps or pattern pieces.

They all had a deep-rooted love for quilting, and this is what bound them; in fact, they were quite passionate about it.

Emma looked out the window at the green countryside, brushing aside a curly hair from her face. She had her quilting purse in her lap, which held an abundant bundle of thread, needles, and her most recent project; however, it contained far from her entire collection of quilting supplies. She hardly went anywhere without her thread purse. It went to the market once a week, to church on Sundays, and even to buy tomatoes from a neighbor that lived nearby-nearby, being several miles from their house and property.

It was hard for her to sit still. She wanted her hands to stay busy with piecing. The nine-patch quilt was easy to work on when they were on the boat, but on the bumpy stagecoach it was simply an unworkable notion. She had tried over and over, only to have the needle prick her finger every tiny jolt. The blood was getting on her blocks. She used her saliva to remove the bloodstains, but her mouth had dried up from the dusty paths they had traveled. She decided finally to place the pieces back into her bag.

"I wish you would not spit on the fabric Emma, it is not very ladylike. Thank you for putting it up."

"Heaven forbid us not be ladylike." Emma said to herself, almost silently.

She crossed her legs again and glanced over to her sister, who was sitting tall against the back of the seat, but then again she was taller than her. Emma was of a medium height, about nineteen years old, with long brownish hair; though when the sunlight shone just right, it was surprising to see just how blonde it really was. Her face was pleasant looking, her eyes green and reflective, and she tended to be rather emotional about things, what's more, almost "outspoken," as they sometimes called her-which bothered her intensely. Her older sister, Abby, was reasonably different from her on many levels and trails. Abby was generally calm, more composed. She was older, about twenty-four, with dark and wavy hair. She was above average height and thin, with wise brown eyes and high cheekbones. Especially notable were her lips that pouted when she was thinking, or when she got angry.

Even though they were both rather different from each other, somehow, they had learned to love and respect each other for their differences. They rarely fought. Though sometimes, if they were to get into a serious discussion about a matter, it appeared to others that they were quarreling; but, in fact, they were oddly enjoying each other, like only sisters can do.

The stagecoach horses pulled over the final rise in the earth that separated them from Lecompte. After five days, they were finally there, and very excited about it.

The town's people could be seen as they busied themselves along the two dusty roads that crisscrossed at the center of town. Liz and Megan stood in front of the market, waiting anxiously in their elegant, puffy dresses. They were both full of anticipation. They moved and wiggled more than two grown ladies should-and felt silly for it-but it couldn't be stopped.

"Oh, I think I see their stage Lizzie," Megan said with girlish excitement. She jumped and squeezed Liz's gloved hand.

"Don't squeeze my hand so hard. That hurt!"

"Sorry Liz, I'm excited is all."

"Oh! There it is, I see it now," Liz said, pointing.

As the stage pulled into the stop, they could see Emma and Abby looking through the side window. Megan immediately rushed over to the stage. Liz followed behind, holding her dress so her feet and legs could move more speedily.

Abby and Emma stepped down the ladder and onto the dirt roadway, from the hot stiff air, to the hot dusty air. And there they were, the Southern cousins, the Mississippi granddaughters, the Wilkes' sisters, in Sunday dresses with pinned hats in their hair and fans in their hands. With Texas-sized dreams in their wicker-woven carry bags and fabric for future quilting projects that would take place on the trail. With love and tired faces, they saw their family members, who had come to greet them. They hugged tightly, assuring them that they looked wonderful and not as though they shown one bit of the five days journey on their faces.

"Oh! Your hair is longer!"

"Is that a new hat?"

"I adore such a dress!"

Town heads turned. Faces looked over with curiously confused expressions. *"Well, what is all the hurly-burly about?"* they seemed to say.

As the ladies were chatting and hugging for a third and fourth time, Grandpa Lucas and Chet, one of the mill workers, were grabbing large trunks and wicker-woven bags and carrying them over to the wagon to be loaded. Each of them took several loads to the wagon, back and forth, back and forth. Finally, once the trunks were loaded, the two men turned towards each other and then to the trunks that laid in the wagon. With looks of mild exasperation, they smiled slightly and shook their heads at the ground. Neither said anything. No words were needed, they understood each other perfectly. It was in their faces, and it said, *"How many trunks could possibly be necessary?"*

All the extra bags especially perturbed Grandpa Lucas, yet he found it humorous all the same. He chuckled jollily at his granddaughters and shook his head at the dirt.

He was once known for having traveled three days on horseback with only a hat and two small loafs of cornbread. Though, nobody was completely sure if it were true or not. Nevertheless, he maintained it as a fact from his "younger years." His horse 'knew the truth,' was his favorite response.

The four ladies thanked the men for their help and then walked down the boardwalk, happily chatting along the way. They had decided to find a place where they could drink tea and enjoy the nice weather.

From the right side of the walkway and on the dirt road, horses were tied up to the log posts stationed in front of every window. Several uncovered wagons were riding along the main road, with dressed-up passengers on board. For a small town, it was actually rather busy during the mornings and afternoons. Each person walking the streets appeared to have serious matters that they must attend to, and couldn't be delayed. They walked quickly with funny looks on their faces.

Abby and Emma were intrigued by the small town's bustle. The relentless whimpering of horses, as they breathed through their nostrils and called to their owners could be heard. They clopped their hooves and looked around, angry to be tied up in such great riding conditions. Wagon wheels rolled over small rocks and crunched as they drove past. A brown horse with sporadic white spotting made eye contact with Emma and watched her as she walked past. He let out a stern huff and stamped his hoof. Emma ignored him and walked on. She was preoccupied looking inside the shop windows at the fancy shawls and dress hats displayed elegantly from their boxes. She had always loved horses, though; and for as long as she could remember, every summer, her family had ridden horses together. She had always loved it. Her father had always told her that "they're smarter than what most people realize," and she believed him. She glanced back at the horse and winked at him.

Grandpa Lucas wandered over to the feed store and found a few grain salesmen to discuss local politics with, one of his favorite diversions.

Meanwhile, Chet was walking down the wooden sidewalk that wrapped in front of the town's stores, nails squeaking as he walked. He couldn't help but watch the rustle of four long skirts as they swished towards the tearoom. The four cousins were walking towards Granny Smith's for afternoon pastries and spiced tea.

He leaped from the boards and pulled out his handkerchief, folding it carefully and then dipping the end of it into the horse trough. He wiped his face and neck, and then put the damp cloth into his back pocket. He reckoned that he too needed something to drink, but they didn't serve his drink of choice at Granny Smith's Tearoom. The saloon had what he needed, and was merely down the street a bit and across a short way. He decided to walk there.

Chet was a born Texan. He had moved to Louisiana when he was twenty-two, for no particular reason. He had sort of stumbled upon Lecompte. A few weeks later he met Lucas and began working at the mill. It was good work, and he knew it. He was respected by all and paid well, but he desperately wanted to go back to Texas. It was in his blood, he had to return. Weeks earlier, he had wanted to ask Lucas if he could be an escort for the girls. He could make sure that they didn't stumble upon trouble-plus, he had trail experience-but he never found the courage to bring it up, and Lucas never asked.

"Whiskey," he called out to the short bartender as he strolled through the swinging doors.

It was now late in the afternoon and few costumers loitered about inside the saloon.

"Ay Chet," someone called from behind him.

Chet turned and searched for the voice that called his name, grinning.

Some of his friends, whom he knew only from the saloon, were sitting in the corner, close to the window. He didn't know most of their names, but somehow, they knew his.

"Thirsty from all of the heavy lifting?" One teased.

Chet looked at them and grinned, shaking his head at the floor.

"Granddaughters of Lucas eh. More of 'em?" another asked.

"Yeh, from Mississippi."

"Hmm, well how long were they gunna be here?"

"Not long. Next week, they leave for Texas."

"Fer Texas!" One said. "Hmmm."

Chet nodded his head.

"They marr'd?"

"I don't know."

"You think they'd wanna marry a fella like me?"

"Ha! Not even if you were willing to leave for Texas in a week!" Chet said, chuckling.

"Wail," he looked down at his whiskey, "maybe I'd go."

Chet laughed and gulped down his whiskey. He motioned for the bartender to pour another and then grabbed a stool next to his saloon-friends.

F ROM THE BOARDWALK, the ladies were opening the door that led into the tearoom. A bell dangling from the door made clunky ringing sounds as they walked through. Inside, the smell was like a bakery-which made Abby remember just how hungry she was.

Emma rubbed her leg that was sore from the trip. For two days, it had hit the side of the stage and was now tender and bruised. Abby too, was relieved to finally be off the stagecoach; but now, they were both tired from the trip, and their faces showed it. Little half moons hung under their eyes and paraded their fatigue around like a little girl in a fancy dress. They felt horrible, mostly from the poor sleeping conditions. The half hour of excitement had disguised their tiredness, and now, as normalness set in; it was easy to notice their exhaustion.

From where the ladies sat, a white linen cloth covered the table. A small candle sat in the middle.

*A tea candle for a tearoom.*

They ordered dessert and tea and immediately began chatting away. The hot air was bursting with thoughts and things to say and discuss. They pulled them down, one by one, trying to get hold of everything that was worth discussing, and many things that didn't matter and weren't worth discussing but got discussed anyway. They chatted about everything that had happened to them since they had last exchanged letters. They were brought up on all of the latest, including most of the plans that they had for their journey west. They talked about future and recent quilting projects, wagons, flowers, men, and lacy hats and hairstyles.

Megan told Abby that she had been offered a teaching job, but the half moons that gathered under her eyes wouldn't allow her to enjoy the moment. She was ecstatic about the news, to say the least, but too exhausted to show it.

At a break in the conversation, Abby pulled her thin gloves off and looked over at Liz. It was hot, and Abby wasn't accustomed to such heat. Liz had been watching her the whole time, and she could tell that something was a matter. She took a sip of her tea and prepared to ask her.

"Abby, is everything all right?"

"Ooh, is it hot in here? It seems very hot."

"Yes, it is warm in here. Take off your hat…here," Liz took her hat and placed it on her lap.

"I suppose I'm just tired or hungry maybe."

"Abby, you don't feel well?" Megan asked. "We could take you home."

"No, I don't want to ruin your plans. I'm fine."

"They really have good food here. I just thought it would be nice if we came here to eat and have some tea."

"No Liz," Abby said. "It is a fine idea. Let's order more tea."

"I'm sorry," Liz said apologetically. "I should have considered that you both would be tired."

"No, no; we will stay here. I'm fine…really."

"You're sure," Liz pressed.

"Yes, I'm sure."

"At least have some water then."

"Thank you."

"Yes, good idea. Have some water," Megan said.

Abby took a big drink of her water and placed her hat back over her head.

"This tea is fantastic," Emma said. "Very tasty."

"Isn't it great," Liz said. "Betty, the owner here, she gets it from New Orleans once a week."

"Yes," Megan said, "her tea is quite famous in Lecompte, everybody loves it."

Abby and Emma were fascinated by Betty.

*Who would've thought of a tea shipment every week? What a wonderful idea of Betty's.*

Chet walked cautiously into the tearoom, just as the ladies were finishing the last of the crumbly pastries. He walked crookedly, but nothing that the women could notice. He touched his hat with confidence and stepped towards the ladies' table.

"Hello Chet," Liz said cheerfully. "What perfect timing. We were about to leave."

Chet wasn't sure what to say. He just smiled.

The ladies stared at him and admired his appearance. He looked handsome in his brown cowboy hat and green button-down. His boots were dark from wear and slightly dusty.

"I would like for you to meet my cousins, Chet. This is Abby," she said, gesturing to Abby. "And this is Emma, her younger sister."

"Ma'am, ma'am," he said, tipping the brim of his hat twice.

"Nice to meet you," they both said, almost in unison.

"Nice to meet you also. Well, I will be out front with the wagon when you ladies are ready to leave."

"Fine then, thank you Chet," Liz said.

He smiled towards Emma, and gave her an extra "Ma'am," as he headed out the door.

Emma smiled back, her cheeks blushing red.

"Oh!" Megan said. "I think that Chet is sweet on you Emma."

"No…really? You think so?"

"Yes, really."

"Maybe so Emma," Liz teased. "I saw the way he looked at you."
Emma looked dazed and slightly embarrassed. "Who is Chet again?"
Megan giggled. "He works at the mill. You will see him again later, I'm
sure."

"Oh!"

They all laughed again and stood to leave. Liz quickly paid with the
money that Lucas had given her, and they walked out to meet the men
at the wagon, who were chewing tobacco with their hands in their
pockets.

Abby and Emma followed slowly behind, thinking that before
bedtime a warm bath would be just what they needed.

# Chapter 6
## *Grandpa's Plan*

A BRIGHT WARM SUN GREETED the Mailly's house the next morning; its light fell over the front porch and through the front windows, making everyone in the house aware that it was out and that it was going to be a lovely day. The sky was mostly clear, except for a few puffy clouds that flit around overhead, and there was virtually no wind at all.

Spring at its peak finest.

As took place almost every morning, Thomas walked through the back door and greeted Grandpa Lucas and Luke, who, in complete silence, were eating breakfast at the kitchen table.

Bacon and strong coffee.

He grabbed a cup and sat down to join them, testing the coffee's temperature with his finger.

*Too hot to drink.*

Unlike most mornings, however, there were now four women living in the house, not the mere two as before. Double the ladies, which meant double the giggling from the porch and sipping of tea after lunch, and double the number of nice looking women that he was used to seeing around the house. Naturally, he didn't have a problem with this. It was far from a disturbance in his opinion. Megan and Abby walked downstairs for breakfast; they could smell the salty bacon from their rooms.

With a great deal of work to begin and finish, the ladies were already dressed and ready to start the day. Many things needed to be finished before they would be ready for the trip. The dishes needed to be packed, the trunks filled, glass cups were to be stuffed with old cloths so they didn't break along the rocky trail. There was a lot to do before they would be ready for the journey west, and they knew that they would be pressed for time to complete it all.

A few months before, Grandpa Lucas had spoken to the stage director in town and calculated that the journey would take four weeks by covered wagon, but maybe longer depending on the weather. 'The heat would be fierce,' he was told, and they should stay close to water for as long as they could. They might have to take individual scouting trips for water if they were unable to find any along their trail. Originally, Grandpa Lucas had not expected the trip to be made during the hot months before summer, but it had worked out that way; and now, he felt obligated to stick with his plan. After all, it was essentially war that they were fleeing from, which, according to his assessment months before, would devastate the mill's operation. He had a very keen understanding of politics in the region, and for that matter, throughout all of the states. He read a national newspaper as often as he could buy one, and in some ways, he was a sort of conspiracist.

*Not a socialist.*

He knew now that gold was what he needed, some of which he had, but they would need more in order to resettle. His idea was essentially that gold would be more stable than any other currency for relocating, especially during war.

About six months before, through correspondence of several letters, Grandpa Lucas was able to buy a large portion of land that was east of Fort Worth and west of Dallas-the small town near the Preston Trail that boasted a hotel and a barbershop.

Liz thought Dallas sounded like a grand city with railways and gold diggers, like a place she had read about in one of Grandpa's newspapers. A place where adventure saturated each day and Indians roamed the mountains and valleys. And even though there were some Indians there, Dallas was really nothing more than a small trading town that bordered the Trinity River. In fact, Lecompte was probably more exciting, but they hadn't realized this yet and hoped for the best.

The area of land that Grandpa Lucas had purchased, so he was told, would be perfect for a house and market if he chose to build one. The land was ideal for farming or operating a ranch-a dream Grandpa Lucas had had for years, even since childhood. And though he was almost seventy years old now, he still hadn't given up on his dream.

Grandpa Lucas was in surprisingly good shape for a man of his age, the repayment for a lifetime's uncompromising workman. He had many years ahead of him, simply because he refused to not stay active. Even now, he still put out nearly the same amount of work he had in his prime. Of course, he had to try harder for the smaller things, but he hadn't given up on his dream. He wanted to follow it, take it in his hand, and live it out. He dreamed of owning a ranch and a small mercantile where his granddaughters could work. He dreamed of open territory that was unspoiled and green, someplace unchanged and untouched, where bison roamed and stallions galloped. He couldn't wait to get there.

The only problem was that he would have to sell the mill in order for his plan to work successfully. His only way of life, since childhood, would be changed. The family mill would be sold and abandoned, and the only thing that he had really ever known would be different. He just wouldn't have enough money otherwise.

All of this frightened Grandpa Lucas a great deal. It kept him from sleeping at night. But he considered himself a man of risk, and he knew what it was he wanted and how to get it. He wanted to take a chance on something that he wasn't sure of. 'This is what life is all about,' he had told Luke just weeks before. To see if a dream would spread its wings and take flight, or close them and come crashing to the ground in a dusty mayhem. Regardless though, whatever might develop or whatever he was dealt, he knew that the mill had to be sold, and his way of life would change forever. He could never go back.

Elizabeth walked downstairs and into the kitchen, adjusting her new hair combs that she had been given by her cousins. She used them to pull her hair back, which meant that it was a workday. She wore her blue cotton dress with a crocheted collar; she held her garden hat in her hand.

She walked over to the cupboard to prepare her breakfast. Grandpa had cooked bacon for everyone, because he couldn't sleep the night before.

*Thinking about the trip.*

Breakfast was black coffee and bacon. A fine breakfast for the men, but the ladies needed warm bread and fruit preserves to start their day, and tea, of course.

Their grandmother had always made her own fruit preserves and had taught them her method before she died. It was a recipe handed down for generations. Their grandmother had always made strawberry, but they had adjusted the recipe to include blackberry or peach. There was only a little left, and with four now eating from the jar, the rest of the dark purple delight wouldn't last a week.

"We've almost finished all of the blackberry," Megan said.

"I know," Liz said, surprised.

"We should grow our own blackberries again," Megan said, "when we get to Texas."

"Do you think they'll grow in Texas?" Emma asked.

"Well," Abby said. "We grew strawberries in Mississippi just fine."

"Surely they will grow," Megan said. "Don't you think Liz?"

"I don't know for certain, but I can't imagine breakfast without blackberry jam."

"Yes, that certainly would be dreadful."

They all looked down at the generous layer of jam that carefully covered each slice of warm bread.

"Well," Liz said, "we can buy some at the market before we leave."

"We could very easily do that," Megan said.

"A lovely idea," Abby agreed.

Thomas smiled at Luke as they watched and listened to the jam conversation between the women. Luke picked up the jar of sticky-purpleness to see just how much was really left. They would miss the berry-picking season in Lecompte.

Grandpa Lucas asked for everyone's attention. The women, now quiet, gave their Grandfather the attention he requested.

Lucas began. "Abby, Thomas brought word this morning, that your cousin Sadie and her friend Alison are not coming. Here is the letter he sent me, you can keep it." Grandpa continued. "We have eight wagons, full of supplies to drive. So I have hired John and Blue from the mill to help drive the two extra teams. Chet, who you've met already, is from Texas and knows the area well. He will ride scout for us."

His granddaughters listened carefully as he spoke.

Abby picked up her teacup to help wash down the warm bread. "Grandpa," she said. "I wish Sadie and Alison would come, but I never

43

thought Uncle James would let his daughters leave with us. And have no confusion on this account; I do not intend to be disrespectful to daddy's family. Grandfather, you have always treated us with respect; and encouraged us to be educated and hold our own opinions. We are ladies and enjoy being women, but we know how to handle guns and drive a team of horses. We are not afraid of hard work. There are many things which we can handle, but some of which I'm not so sure. I am certain that I speak for all of us about our excitement for the trip, but it's something which I've been thinking about, and I must say that I am rather concerned about the case for Indians." Abby caught her breath.

The group looked to Lucas.

"Abby, I confess I am greatly worried over this issue. There is little we can do to prevent a raid. Of course, we would never provoke them and always be on guard. You will always need to stay together, always." He reiterated. "I have been in contact with a Texas Ranger. A small group of them are going to meet up with you at the border and help you get to the fort. With Thomas, Chet and the Rangers, there is nothing else we can forestall. These are good men and I trust they will do a fine job of protecting you."

Abby felt a little better, but suddenly, she did not know which scared her the most; the thought of Indians or her new classroom.

"You know," Grandpa Lucas started again, "that I will be there as soon as the sale of the mill is finalized. The new owners need to be comfortable before I can leave. I feel this is the respectable manner to address the new owners. Also, the land contract in Pineville will need to be finalized for the purpose of logging rights. This should occur so that I arrive in the fall."

Thomas stood to retrieve the coffee pot again.

"The general store will need supplies. There is no freight coming in once the army moves west. The army that built and used the fort is now abandoning their garrisons. As we all know, whoever arrives first will hold ownership. If enough people take over the responsibilities

44

then we rightly have the making of a town. I have decided to try and make a-go of the freight lines. Perhaps, John and Blue will stay with me and become drivers. Though, I've not yet discussed this with them."

Luke squirmed in his chair. The excitement was more than he could handle. He had never dreamed of such adventure.

"We will start packing today," Grandpa Lucas stated. "It will be a lot of work to fit it all in, but we can do it."

Liz adjusted her new hair combs and smiled at her grandfather as she prepared for the day's work.

"Well, let's get started," Megan announced.

"HOW SHALL WE START?" Abby asked Liz. "I thought you and Megan could start here in the kitchen. Only leave the minimum. Grandpa will have most of his meals at the mill with the other men. The sawdust and wooden crates are stacked in the breezeway. Pack the breakables in the sawdust and nail each lid down well." Liz instructed. "Also, think about what we will need the next few days. We can pack those items right before we leave. We want to take as much as we can on this trip. Grandpa will only bring what he has to, because all of his wagons will be freight."

Emma and Megan swished out the door to the breezeway. Emma was gathering several of the crates from the porch while Megan struggled with a heavy bag of sawdust. She tugged with frustration on the sturdy burlap, but it would not budge. She stepped away from the bag and placed her hands tightly against her hips. Her hair was now damp at the temples from the morning's sun, which beamed straight through the open porch with intensity.

Emma appeared and tapped her on the shoulder with a giggle

"This bowl and small bag may help lighten the load." She laughed as she handed it to her cousin.

"Don't laugh. I would have figured it out. I never thought these little pieces of tree dust could cause me such trouble."

Megan began to scoop the sawdust into the bag. She stopped to wipe her hair away from her eyes. She would have to remember to firmly secure her hair in the future. This style would never work on the wagon trail. She made a quick adjustment with a few pins and went back to work. With the bag of sawdust now workable, Megan brought it into the kitchen where she and Emma chatted while carefully packing their heirlooms.

Abby headed to the cellar to retrieve the canned goods. The door creaked open and dusty sunrays ran ahead of her down the stairs. The dark place began to fill with light as she gathered her skirt and entered the coolness. Cobwebs hung carelessly and hit Abby in the face. She blinked trying to adjust to the new surroundings. Wooden shelves were on all sides bulging with stone crocks and canned goods. The pantry was filled with peaches, dried apples, tomatoes and several sacks of onions and potatoes. The Mailly's were excellent gardeners and they were equally blessed in their canning skills. Abby found a stockpile of the special jam that had caused such a stir at breakfast. They would not have to worry about a berry patch in Texas for a while. She laughed as she thought about the look on young Luke's face.

Even though it was the end of the season, the cellar was full. Liz and Megan had prepared their harvest well. Abby realized that she had a great deal to learn from her cousins. In many ways, they had grown into women of confidence since she had last seen them; in other ways, she admired them for their independence that they had achieved in spite of not having a livelihood through placement, as she did. Abby had aspired to attain such independence as a teacher, but she now realized that it came from poise and not from vocation.

Abby began to sort the abundance into categories. The shelf closest to the stairs will be for grandpa. She placed a sack of coffee beans and an extra jar of peaches next to the other items that Liz had requested. As she looked at the shelf, it looked like more than her grandfather would need, especially if he were to take his meals at the mill with the other workers.

She looked to her paper that Liz had given her with the allotments. Next, she placed on the shelf below grandpa's the items that they would need in the next few days. The butter crock, a small block of cheese, jam and another crock that held salt were lined up next to the others.

Abby was impressed with Liz's organization. There would certainly be plenty of food for the trip and an amount sufficient enough to start their new home. She had to hand it to her cousin; Liz was very prepared for their journey.

"Perhaps," she thought, "this trip will not be too taxing after all."

Abby glanced at Liz's list for the other items to pack. She had it in two columns: food that would stay packed for future Texas use, and that which they would eat on the trail. With eight mouths, the trail-food could go quickly. Their plan was to eat what they could find along the way-as much as possible.

After the food was sorted, Abby went up the stairs to the crates and sawdust. It was a great day, not too warm yet. The birds seemed unusually happy.

As Abby approached the top of the stairs, she saw Liz giving instructions to John and Blue-whom were struggling to lift some heavy, prepacked boxes into the freight wagons. Liz was particular in the way she wanted these wagons packed; it had to be just so.

"Miss Elizabeth, we can never get all of this in these wagons." John wiped the trickle that went by is eye and took one glove off as he tried to explain the situation to the unsurrendering female.

"John, I do not wish to be difficult, but if you would just try it this way. I am certain it will fit. See, I have it all planned out here." She pushed the paper toward John.

He took the paper and reluctantly looked it over.

Abby caught Liz's eye and motioned her over.

"Is everything all right?" She asked concerned

"Yes," Liz firmly stated, "as soon as he completes it my way."

They laughed gently and stared over to the wagon area. Liz could see that John had arranged the boxes her way and they were beginning to fit, rather amazingly, into their predestined locations.

A short while later, everyone agreed that it was lunchtime. It was a good time to see how they were doing with the list Liz had given them.

As Liz and Abby approached the kitchen area, laughter could be heard from the two inside.

"What is so funny dear sister?" Abby asked Emma.

Coming up for air Emma stumbled with her words. Megan came to her aid and said. "She was telling me about the school picnic and the gift you received," Megan giggled again.

"Oh, I don't want to even think about little Samuel and the snake!" Abby waved her hands and changed the topic. "I've worked up such an appetite in that cellar with all of that food. I must eat something! And by the way Liz, you and Megan have really outdone yourselves. The cellar is packed with jar after jar. Emma you would not believe it. Here is the most beautiful jar of pickles I have ever seen. Did you ever enter these in the county fair, by the way?"

"Yes, we did in fact; and we gained several new enemies throughout the county." Megan teased. "Grandma Claire always had the purple ribbon till we came along. Lonnie Gluffer said his wife was right glad we're leaving; she just might have a chance at it now."

"Oh my then! These must be worth a lovely fortune." Abby held the jar high and admired it as the light caressed the shinny glass.

Secret spices and seeds floated in and around the perfect slices of little cucumbers.

Suddenly, the ladies all heard the casual footsteps of boots on the porch. Thomas had thought that he was a lucky man to be in charge of this mostly female group, until he spoke with John and Blue out on the breezeway. Thomas happened to come by when the latter two were complaining about the bossy women, and how, they only knew how to do the packing just so; and that the men did not. Liz had told them to use her celestial list and pack accordingly. Thomas smiled; just then, he decided to use a more soft approach with Liz. He had seen his friend Caleb wind up on the losing end with her many a time. As he looked at her smiling and enjoying herself, he now understood why Caleb had no trouble at all dealing with this.

Finally, he opened the door with cautioned confidence and entered the kitchen. "Hello ladies, how is all with the packing?" He asked himself already aware of the male side of the story. "Looks like the family pickle secret is about to be shared. Should I come back?"

"Of course not, come in." Megan smiled. "We will never tell. We were about to have some lunch. Won't you join us?"

"Thank you, but I have a lot to do today. Liz, can I see you on the porch for a moment?"

Thomas held the door open for Liz and they both left the room. The others looked confused.

Megan looked at Abby with a strange face.

"They look so nice together. What is their matter?" Abby asked.

"Short and simple is the fact that he won't approach her as more than a family friend. You know someone who simply cares and nothing more. Sadly, she loves Caleb still." Megan stated

"So then," Emma asked, confused, "if he would only make his intentions known…it would change things?"

"Well, not entirely." Megan began to explain. "Thomas feels loyalty to his best friend and he doesn't want to push Liz if she is not keen to accept callers."

"Well!" Emma exclaimed. "This could go on forever, the waiting and waiting!"

"Exactly." Megan sighed. "I have tried to nudge Liz into seeing otherwise; it falls on deaf ears."

"Well," Abby said. "I suppose it hasn't even been a year."

Outside on the porch, Thomas struggled with Liz seeing his point of view.

"Thomas, I can't imagine the problem with John." She stated firmly. "It's quite simple. The crates were not fitting in the wagon as I had planned and it was because he wanted to do it his way. We have a lot to pack and it will not all fit if such things are not considered. I even had the crates made a certain size so that we would not waste one lovely inch of room in the wagons. If they do not place them as I have recorded on the sheet of paper, it simply won't work. I did it to save them time and trouble.

"I think they would have figured it out Liz, if you had let them."

"But why should they waste time figuring this out when I already have?" She asked, not really seeking a response. "They would then tell me I couldn't take all the items and that is unacceptable. The breezeway would be full of crates, which no place were suited for," she paused. "I would load all this myself if it were not so heavy."

Liz began to feel hot for some reason. Thomas questioning her made her mad. She had done nothing but organize all of the wagons. Their life may depend on what she made room for and where she chose to store it. Megan was to start her dress shop and had to have her supplies, as well as, the inventory for the mercantile. This was no easy task that her grandfather had given her.

"Let's not pretend. The real problem is that I told them what to do and he wouldn't have it." Liz stared at Thomas.

Thomas didn't answer.

"Am I not right? Are the crates fitting?" Liz held her ground like an animal defending her young, her lace-up boots pressed firmly against the porch.

Thomas looked over to the two freight wagons that were beginning to gain weight. The crates appeared to fit in their places, with little wasted space. He looked to the covered porch to estimate the space for the remaining freight.

"All right then. Well, I will have a word." Thomas walked down the steps.

Liz walked quickly back to the kitchen. "Men!" she exclaimed as she walked through the doors.

Thomas stood by the wagons and examined the final boxes, which waited for loading.

"You came out well on that one." Blue groaned as he lifted one of the crates into the wagon.

Thomas remained silent.

"What does she have in this one?" Blue complained. "I might need a hand here fellas."

"No, this one? It mustn't be that heavy. It says Megan's fabric on the side." John answered back, confused. He wiped the sweat from his face and neck with his red bandana.

"Well, it's rather heavy I'm telling you."

Thomas looked to the boxes on the porch that still waited to be placed in the wagon. On the side of each box, in bold lettering, was written:

Megan's Fabric - Freight wagon 2

"Life or death," Thomas remembered Liz saying.
It would be his life if any of it were left behind.

"Fellas, don't forget any of these." Thomas reminded the men. Thomas swung his leg over the back of his horse and rode away. He had rather enjoyed the little joust with Liz.

## Chapter 7
## The Women on the Porch

SEVERAL DAYS HAD PASSED and the wagons began to groan as they adjusted to their new weight. Time had passed quickly and all was now loaded except for Megan's treadle machine. A special area had been made for it with ties to hold it in place and to keep it from moving around on the trail.

The work had taken less time than Liz had anticipated. She felt relieved that they would leave on time. The ladies would take a break all afternoon to finish their personal agendas and rest some. If there were time, they planned to quilt around the old frame; otherwise, they would get an early start and quilt the next day.

Liz and Abby sat in their rockers on the porch. Megan stood by the treadle machine, which waited patiently next to the wagon. Emma sat in a straight back chair with quilt blocks in her lap. All of the square patch units were complete and she was piecing the triangle units that would go on the sides. Two triangle pieces were sewn to a red square, which created a large triangle unit that was then sewn to the nine-patch. The fabric was consistent throughout the quilt except for the center squares that varied in shades of red or green. Emma was at her best with a needle and fabric in her hand. She was calm and at ease with the world. They rocked and waited for the men to load the treadle in utter silence.

Abby broke into their thoughts. "I have something for everyone. Being the schoolteacher that I am, I thought we should record our trip west." She reached into her apron pocket and took out a little journal for each one of them. "I have already started mine. In fact, I've been keeping one since I went away to teaching school. We should do it for ourselves, but for history, too." Abby handed a small pencil to each one just as she had done a thousand times in her classroom. Abby was a natural teacher-encouraging, patient and persistent. Her teacher-eyes were kind and imploring. "Write whatever you wish, it is your story."

Megan was first to respond and as always, excited about something new. "How exciting! I've never kept a diary before."

"Yes, Abby, what a lovely idea. I would have never of thought of it myself." Liz agreed.

Emma placed her book in her sewing bag at the side of her chair. She quickly picked up her needle again and got back to her stitching. "Thank you," she said indifferently.

"Oh, come now Emma. It will be fun!" Megan begged her cousin.

The ladies rocked in silence and waited for the muscle to arrive and load the treadle-except for Megan; she paced around the machine like a mother hen. She wouldn't have her treadle placed haphazardly.

54

# Chapter 8
## Needles a-Smoking

THE LADIES COMPLETED THEIR MORNING ROUTINE in record
time and hastily made their way into the sewing room, which
was actually an extra room that nobody had ever used for
anything. It had one large window and a small closet that had been
turned into a bookshelf. The floors were wood and still looked new, as
though they had somehow escaped the passage of time, for they were
never walked on and never used.

A large, yellow cat slowly pranced across the floor in front of
Emma, rubbing up against her leg.

"Oh! I can't wait to get started on this quilt." Abby said.

"Where have you been hiding?" Emma said, reaching down to pet
the plump, yellow ball of fur.

"That's Samson." Megan said. "He's very old."

"Oh," Emma said. "Well, aren't you just the most charming ole fellow," she said in a strange baby voice. "Where have you been?"

The women had grown anxious to quilt, for the last few days were filled with loading and work, and there was no time left for quilting. They quickly gathered around the quilt frame with their sewing baskets and started at once.

Abby licked the eye of her needle and pressed the heavy cotton thread into it.

Megan was watching Abby's technique. "I thought you licked the thread, not the needle, to help you thread it quickly,"

"Well, you can, I suppose; but a friend of mothers always said to do it this way." Abby smiled.

Each seamstress was eager to try this new hint. One by one, they placed the eye of the needle between their lips to moisten the opening and then pointed the tip of the thread into the metal opening of the needle. All three of the needles were threaded the first time with no trouble.

"Isn't that wonderful!" Megan exclaimed.

The quilt top that they were working on was not especially big. Megan called it a lap size because it was just large enough to cover a person when seated.

Emma was quite taken with this smaller version. She even thought it could hang on the wall like a picture. They all were amused over a quilt that would hang on the wall. Its only purpose would be a source of beauty, a wall decoration-which seemed to be a rather astonishing idea.

The quilt was layered with cotton batting in the middle and a muslin length of cloth would cover the back. It was stretched tightly in the wooden frame. It would be completed quickly since it was a smaller piece of appliqué art, and because, four talented hands would be flying across it.

Each needle was threaded with a knot at the end of the thread, except for Liz's. She never used a knot; instead, she used a double backstitch for each time she started a line of stitches. The eye of the needle allowed the thread to move through it without hindrance as each stitch was worked into the quilt.

The needle was pushed into the middle layer of the batting and pulled through tightly, popping the knot into the batting and between the layers of the quilt sandwich. An accomplished quilter would never allow a knot to show on either side of the quilt. Each seamstress at this quilt frame was an expert with the needle. Abby and Emma were taught the art of the needle by their mother, Katherine-who was the youngest daughter of Lucas Mailly. Elizabeth and Megan were taught by their grandmother, Claire.

The women in the community were always excited to go to a quilt gathering. They might be called a-quilt'n or a quilting bee. A quilt could be finished rather quickly with so many hands at work. Sewing secrets were passed around, as well as, community news and activities-not to be confused with local gossip, which the church gatherings frowned upon. One brass woman from the saloon referred to the gatherings as the local *stitch and bitch*. When Megan had heard this reference to the gathering it made her forehead wrinkle. She had never been to anything that would resemble such a group.

"I will certainly miss our little group of quilting friends," Megan said to Liz.

"Yes, such a lovely group of friends here!"

"Perchance, we can assemble another."

"I suppose so; but how could it be as memorable?"

"Well," Emma chimed in, "maybe it will be even better."

Row after row, the thimbled-fingers loaded stitches into the appliquéd, flower pattern quilt. The ladies rolled the quilt several times as the work progressed. It was a pattern which their grandmother Claire had designed a myriad of years ago; for this reason, it was special to all of them.

Liz and Emma were still concentrating on their stitches, twelve to the inch to be exact.

Two gray kittens play with each other; they swatted and jumped at Samson's tail, which had a mind of its own. Another kitten curled around Abby's leg under the quilt frame and rolled itself in her skirt that looked like a gossamer puddle on the floor.

Emma and Megan quickly disappeared to retrieve lunch.

Liz was finally at the end of her thread. She slid the needle under the top layer of fabric and secured a backstitch to the cotton batting. She pulled out her stork embroidery scissors and neatly clipped the thread. She then placed her needle into the edge of the spool. "We certainly have accomplished a lot this morning," she said, looking the quilt over with her fingers and eyes. Her fingers smoothed over the tiny stitches she had just placed in the quilt. "It is coming along nicely," she said mostly to herself.

The playful kitten suddenly jumped into her lap, briefly scaring her. "Cally, you silly thing. I sure will miss you," she stroked the soft fur and held the kitten to her face.

Abby was admiring the woman across from her. She was beautiful with her bright skin and silky hair. She had confidence and courage in her soft heart. Abby had hurt so deeply for her cousin when she heard about Caleb's death. She was happy to see for herself that Liz was recovering.

Liz felt Abby's eyes on her and looked up to the equally beautiful woman. "Abby, I am so glad you are here. It has been far too long. I was beyond excitement to hear that you and Emma were willing to make the move."

Abby reached for Liz's hand across the quilt and smiled gracefully.

"Grandpa is so certain about this political unrest, it is frightful Liz."

"I know." Liz gently squeezed Abby's fingers. "Let's not worry ourselves though. Grandpa seems certain of this and I have faith in him."

"Yes, I do as well. But that doesn't mean that I won't worry."

"Yes, I worry too, but let's not dwell on things we can't change." Liz paused.

Abby nodded in agreement.

"Are you excited about your new teaching engagement? Pastor Parker seems so nice, and his wife, Anna does too."

"Yes, I am. Excited and worried all at once." Abby expelled a deep breath. "I do not know where to begin. I have to be careful to not scare myself into running back to my Mississippi classroom."

"We will take it one day at a time." Liz comforted her with soft words and a soft pat on her hand.

"Liz, I am very curious about Texas and I do not feel that I know much about it. What can you tell me?" Abby pressed. "Settle my nerves."

Liz began, "I understand the weather is actually quite similar as here, hot and such. Only, less trees and rain, which might not be too terrible. We are almost on the edge of what they call west Texas, a most barren place it is. Our area, however, has trees and a river-the Trinity River, to be more specific. Sounds like home almost. Doesn't it? Except they say it's ranch country. It has cattle grazing land and open prairie. Cattle with great long horns roam about all over. Grandpa and Thomas are always talking on the porch about this ranching. Thomas told me that a person could round up as many of these longhorns as they wish, brand them and they are yours!"

Abby smiled.

"The idea of a ranch is very exciting to them. Luke is taken with the idea of being a cowboy. Grandpa forgets how old he is; he never quits and Thomas seems to think that Grandpa too is a young man. Thomas has just stepped into the shoes Caleb wore in Grandpa's life and Luke's too." Liz paused realizing what she had just said.

"Well, what about you Liz? Has he stepped into those shoes for you?" Abby quizzed Liz gently.

"I have not thought about it exactly like that." Liz looked to Abby with tears in her eyes again. She tried to blink them back. "I still feel married, except that I get lonely; my heart just hurts, but I want to feel better. And," she paused, "if forgetting Caleb is what I have to do to get better then I don't see that I can do it. I will never be able to do that."

"I have not been here long my dear cousin, but I can say that Thomas adores you. He doesn't have to court you; he is already here. He is already in this family; and, too, he is a gentleman. He is waiting for you to make room for him in your heart. He won't be assertive, Liz;

but my only advice is to not wait too long for happiness to find you. You shouldn't wait."

Megan and Emma now appeared with sandwiches and lemonade on a tray.

Abby reached for her drink. "We have much work ahead of us. Though much we've already accomplished, there is even more which lies waiting once we reach Texas."

She looked to the others for support.

Emma now leaned forward, propping her elbows on the edge of the quilt frame with her chin in her hands. "I am growing more excited each day. I can barely manage the anticipation. And though it's exciting, a part of me feels frightful too. I only wish Grandpa was coming with us."

Megan was munching something crunchy and prepared to say something. "At first, I also felt frightful, and though it may come again, I have confidence in us. We may be women, but we can do this, I've all but any doubt. It's an opportunity, and as such it will be wonderful!"

The ladies were amused at Megan's outlook.
"Besides," she said, "I've become a wonderful shot!" She raised her hand to look like a revolver and pretended to blow smoke from its barrel.

They all laughed at the charismatic, yet pensive Megan. She sat down, still in an excited state of mind and continued on. "I am most excited at the prospect of having a dress shop. My own new," she emphasized, "treadle machine. Just wait till you see that new treadle sewing machine work. We ordered it from Chicago you know; I paid for it myself. The dresses will simply fly off the machine."

She finally stopped for air and carefully sipped her tea.

Liz smiled at her sister, affirming her words. "It will be a hard life for a while. I don't know how far the water is. We might have to carry it. We might even have to live in our wagons. It certainly won't be as comfortable as we have it here." Liz looked to her family with concern. "We will experience first hand how our grandmothers lived and what their daily life was like."

Emma listened and tried to imagine daily life on the Texas frontier.

# Chapter 9
## Grandpa's Porch

**L**IZ SAT ON HER FRONT PORCH mending the binding on her Grandpa's favorite quilt which he himself had named Southern Skies. It had long thin star points of blue and red. The background was made from tan scraps. He had told Liz that the stars were as big and beautiful as the stars in the Louisiana night sky.

Lucas loved the porch as much as Liz did. When she was a little girl, he had told her the story of the geese flying south for the winter, and the way the birds knew when to fly north or south. He had told her how the birds supported and encouraged each other in the journey. The bird that was in the lead had the hardest job. He had to break the wind currents for the others behind him. Each bird behind the front one had an easier time flying. The flock always flew in the 'V' formation; the last held the resting or coasting spot. They were always squawking as they flew over the Mailly property. Lucas said the birds were voicing support and encouragement to each other. They praised the lead bird for its leadership. When a goose is injured and needs to leave the group, they send down several to aid him in his recovery. They can join up with any flock coming over when the injured bird is ready to fly again.

Grandpa Lucas had always said that people need to be like these creatures, praising the leaders, encouraging others and hardworking.

When Liz made Grandpa's quilt she put twelve flying geese in each block. She told him that it makes her think of the time they had spent on the porch together and what he had taught her about life.

Liz would miss this porch, but it calmed her knowing that her family was going with her and she could build a new one.

She was tired. It had been busy, laborious days. Liz looked at the eight wagons standing packed with goods. The structures looked as if they were ready to give birth.

Birth of a new life was now upon Liz, and she was hearing and feeling the pains of labor. The feelings of happy expectation and fright were both in her belly.

Her family was already in bed. Everyone was as tired as she was, but she was unable to sleep. It seemed she spent many nights on the porch on account of her insomnia.

In the morning, she would leave the Mailly home. She would leave Riverton.

She went to the porch one last time on this night.

In prayer, she thought of God's promises; she asked for wisdom, guidance, health, and safety. She asked for strength and endurance. She was thankful that Thomas would travel all the way with them and that Chet would be their scout. He knew Texas; it was his home.

She sat rocking, comforted by the fact that the Rangers would help guide them in the more dangerous areas.

"Please God," she requested one more time. "Protection, special protection."

"A penny for your thoughts?" Grandpa Lucas asked from the

doorway with his pipe in hand.

Liz looked his way. "I just finished mending your favorite quilt."

"Thank you, Liz. You know how much I love that quilt." He stepped forward, leaning on a post of the porch and lighting his pipe.

She looked down at the flying geese on the quilt.

"These birds are amazing, the way God created their nature…" She looked up to her grandfather and smiled. "How do you know they are squawking encouragement to each other? Maybe they are griping."

Smoke went up from his pipe, his leg crossed over the ankle of the other. His eyes twinkled in the darkness at Liz. He chuckled. "I choose to believe in the good and positive, Liz. Besides, a little bird told me." His eyebrows teased a wiggle.

She stood up, placed the quilt in the rocker and went to her grandfather. With her arms around him she said. "I love you, I miss you already." Her voice cracked. She looked out over his shoulder and blinked back a burn from her eyes.

"Not my shirt again!" He teased. He wrapped his arm around her and smiled.

"Maybe a little melancholy about leaving my home, but I am ready to go. In the morning, I will be ready. Why aren't you in bed?" She asked him.

"I was waiting on my quilt." He chuckled. "Can't sleep without it you know."

She picked it up and placed it in his arms.

"I love you."

"I love you too, Liz. I know you can do it. I will see you soon, real soon. When the birds fly south."

Liz looked back at her Grandpa on the night porch and chiseled it into her heart. She never wanted to lose such memories.

# Chapter 10
## Westward the Women

**L**IZ MUST HAVE FALLEN ASLEEP the very moment her head hit the pillow. She didn't even remember getting into bed or saying her nightly prayer.

The days before were full of packing and planning of final details-which had exhausted her to the core. In a way it was odd that she could sleep so easily, because she was incredibly anxious about the day that waited for her when she would awake. It would be a day unlike any she had every before experienced.

Liz rolled over in the darkness to face the window, her hair in her eyes. She brushed it aside.

"Is it almost morning yet?" she whispered to herself.

She went to the window and peaked out.

"No sun yet."

While she had slept, the moon had glided across the sky and now shown from the opposite side from where she had last seen it. The stars were shining over the house and the eight wagons waited in the yard, awaiting their dusty day ahead where they would be useful and satisfied.

"Today, we go," she thought. "It's really going to happen. At the end of this day, I won't be here anymore or maybe ever again. I'll be someplace else. "

Excitement squeezed her insides. She slipped back into her warm bed and tried to sleep, for she knew that she would regret not having a full night's rest if later she were tired.

A pink ray of sunlight sliced through Liz's morning curtains and splashed against her face and pillow. Within moments, she was in the kitchen preparing a small breakfast and lunch for along the trail. She wrapped a piece of bread and cheese in a small cloth for everyone and then placed it into a larger cloth sack that held two green apples and a tin cup. She made a sack for each person. Once finished, she would place each sack under the wagon bench for the drivers to have later.

For the first day on the trail, cheese would be a real luxury for lunch. Afterwards, it would be impossible to carry such things that could easily spoil in the high temperatures. From then on out, they would have to eat dried meats, breads, and beans; and hopefully, they could kill something for dinner each night. The jars of preserved fruit and other items from the cellar were packed neatly away in the sawdust for special occasions or hard times on the trail. Liz was bringing four chickens that hopefully would produce eggs.

Grandpa was already up, inspecting the wagons once again before they would be trail-worthy. In one wagon, he placed several extra wooden wheels and other materials that might be useful if the originals were damaged during the journey. It was surprisingly easy to break off a wheel. Sometimes the spokes would catch and strip the entire insides away. Or, as happened more often than any other scenario, the bolts would wiggle off and lose hold of the wheel, sending the wagon down in a dusty crash.

Grandpa Lucas had seen this before and wanted to ensure that they would have enough materials for in the instance this did happen— which, as he had told everyone, would probably happen at least once to each wagon.

The group gathered in the kitchen and quickly ate breakfast. Afterwards, they collected all of the essential items that for whatever reason could not be packed the night before and placed them in their appropriate wagons.

Most of the mill workers were waiting in the yard next to the wagons, noticeably intrigued that Grandpa Lucas was actually allowing his four granddaughters to do such a thing.

*How could he allow them to travel to Texas without him?*

It was rather significant to many people of the community that Grandpa Lucas would allow his granddaughters to embark on such a voyage west. Alone. Especially considering that no man to whom they were related was going along. It was a rare occurrence for any woman or group of women to have such an opportunity. In essence, it positioned a stepping-stone in this small community; a stone that, years later, would be stepped on by several other women and used over and over again for days to come.

Luke placed his mother's chickens into her wagon. She surveyed their placement and adjusted their wooden cages as she saw fit. Luke smiled at his mom and gave her a hug.

"They could drop out Luke. It's not going to be trails like we are accustomed to. These trails are much more shaky and not used so often."

"Are you set?" He asked her.

Liz's eyes grew big and she smiled. "Yes, I suppose I am all set."

"Good! I can't wait to get out there! I wonder how far we'll make it today."

"Almost certainly not far." Liz smiled. "Where's Bear?"

"Grandpa has him," he said, motioning towards his grandfather, who was discussing something with Thomas. "Bear! Come boy!" Luke whistled. A big fluffy-haired black ball came running towards Liz and him, stopping just in time. Luke patted his sides and rubbed his head with two hands. "Are you all set boy?" The dog grew more and more excited with Luke's encouraging words. The black dog couldn't take anymore and barked from the taunting. "Good boy," Luke assured him.

The wagons were lined up according to Grandpa Lucas' instructions and stood patiently with drivers now on board. Grandpa had decided that the best manner to travel would be in pairs, meaning that two wagons would travel next to each other and two wagons would travel behind, and so on and so forth. This allowed each person to have a partner that could assist the other if they needed it. So, the wagons were arranged accordingly and Grandpa Lucas was satisfied to have this matter settled in his favor. At least, he could be sure of something.

Thomas would be in front, leading the groups of wagons, and he also agreed that this method of travel was a good idea for in the instance one of the ladies needed help with the reins. Behind his wagon were Liz and Megan, Abby and Emma, Luke and Blue, and John single at the rear. Chet would be on horseback.

*All around and everywhere.*

Thomas had his saddle horse tied to the side of the wagon. Grandpa Lucas mentioned that it was always a good idea to take a few extra horses that would be fresh for when they needed to scout ahead or search for water.

Grandpa Lucas had given all of his granddaughters a final hug and saluted the men with a handshake and a few words of advice. He decided to say a prayer before they left and asked for everyone to join with him. Everyone agreed. He asked that God would keep His hand over the group and guide them in safety and health. His wish was for Thomas' wisdom as the trail leader and for the overall protection of each person.

"Amen," everyone said together as he finished his prayer.

Grandpa Lucas raised his hand to Liz. "Will those chickens be a bother?"

"They won't." Liz said. "They know how much I love chicken soup."

"Aha!" he said, as if realizing something. He looked over. "Thomas!"

"Yes sir?"

"Take my women to Texas!" He called out.

"I will sir!"

For all of the mill workers that stood watching, this moment of excitement was above all they could handle that they immediately started clapping and hollering at the wagons. They waved their hands and shouted goodbyes.

"Yee haw!" Thomas shouted at his horses to start them off.

The wagons began to pull out of the yard while all of the mill workers and Grandpa stood watching and waving. Liz watched the house with her beloved porch and kept thinking that she would never see it again. She stared at the river and then back to her grandfather, who was getting smaller and smaller. She looked to each side as the wagon moved along the road and everything she grew up with.

*Past the huge trees*
*The honeybees.*
*The barn, the mill,*
*Where slopes the grassy hill.*

Finally, they reached the edge of the Mailly property. Liz looked over to Megan, who was so excited that she could hardly stay seated over the wagon bench. Her petite gloved hands driving a team of horses. Liz smiled at her sister. She had always admired her sister's love for life. It was in the small things, the day-to-day matters that she found the most odd satisfaction for living. The special way she held the stem of a flower bulb before placing it carefully into its allotted square hole, or the way she threaded a needle and secured a perfect knot, even the way she cleaned things.

"We're leaving! I can't believe this." Megan exclaimed to Liz, trying to talk over the horses. "We're actually leaving Riverton!"

"I know it! Can you believe I never really dreamed we'd leave here?"

Liz bit her lip and tried to smile back at her sister. That lone tear was finding its way to her chin again. She quickly looked back as she went around the bend in the road. She saw her grandfather on the porch with his hand held high, still waving.

# Chapter 11

## The Hope of Great Beginnings

**T**HE SUN WAS STRAIGHT OVERHEAD now and hot. They had made surprisingly good distance for the time they had been on the trail. The area they saw now was not as familiar to the females; in fact, Abby and Emma had never seen it before.

Chet rode over the crest of a small hill and slowed his horse to the speed of Thomas' wagon. Liz and Megan watched him as he discussed something off to the right side of the wagon, his hands motioning in reference to something. Thomas' head dodged in the direction he was pointing.

"How does it look over there?" Thomas asked

"Still like Louisiana," Chet joked.

"Go back and make sure the others are doing fine. If we can find water, I'd like to stop for the horses."

"Very well. I will tell them."

Chet pushed away from the wagon and rode back a short way to where Liz and Megan's wagons were driving.

"Hello," he called out slowing his horse to their speed. "How is everything?"

"Just fine," Liz said. "Is everything all right?"

"Yes. Everything is fine."

"We saw you and Thomas motioning towards those hills. What were you saying?"

"Oh, nothing important. He would like to stop in an hour for the horses."

"For the horses?" Megan asked. "Why not for us? For the ladies? We have been traveling all day!"

"Well," Chet looked confused. "We will stop for everyone and for lunch as well. We can stretch our legs." He wasn't certain that he had answered her question. "I've to make sure that the others are doing fine. I'll be back." He quickly took off for the wagons behind them in which Abby and Emma were traveling.

Chet slowed his horse and let Emma's wagon catch up to him. He noticed the way she was holding her reins. She was inexperienced, but certainly not incapable. He rode close to the side of her and leaned over the wagon.

"Place the reins in your fingers like this and relax some." He said.

She looked up to Chet who was smiling at her.

"See, that's better."

After Chet had confirmed that each wagon was doing fine, he rode on to relay the news to Thomas.

"Good," Thomas said. "Did you tell them that we would stop soon?"

"Yes, I did. They supposed the sooner the better."

"They need to stop?"

"Yes, I reckon everyone would like a break soon."

"Very well. See if you can scout a place for water."

"We've been traveling parallel to a large creek. Almost six feet across I'd say."

"Really?"

"For about three miles."

"Can you lead the way?"

"Yes, it's only a short way. Follow me!"

The wagons tracked off to the right side with Chet leading the way. Up ahead there was a thick group of low trees, and just beyond that was a rocky area and a flowing creek. Almost six feet across, just as Chet had said.

The wagons came to a halt before reaching the area of thick growth that bordered the creek. There was a wide perch where the horses could enjoy shade and drink water. The ladies quickly unloaded and went for the creek to wash and have a drink of fresh water. Blue, John, and Lucas walked down to the creek-just behind the women-to get water and fill several buckets that the horses could drink from. Chet and Thomas stayed behind, close to the wagons and horses.

"Everything is going well," Chet said.

Thomas took a long drink from his canteen and then pushed the cork lid over the opening. "So far," he said flatly. "It's not what is up there that I have concern about, it's what is traveling behind us."

Chet glanced over his shoulder and down to the creek where the others were washing their faces. "Behind us? What do you mean?"

"Indians." Thomas said, while wiping his mouth.

Chet's face looked concerned, but he tried to hide it. "What did Lucas say about engines?"

"To watch out for them."

"Today even? We've only just started."

"Well, I don't want to ferret out anything about Indians. Make no mistake on that account." He assured Chet. "Especially for the sake of the women."

Chet nodded.

"What I mean is that we are still close to Pineville and the ladies don't seem anxious just yet, but they are women. They could easily change their minds. And really, I have no wish to turn around to Pineville for their sake."

Chet cut in. "Do you really think they would turn back?"

"We should keep a close eye on that for a few days." Thomas propped his arm on the wagon. "We hardly made any distance. It would be easy for them to turn back."

"Yes," Chet agreed. "But it's better than what we'd expected."

Thomas dipped his head in agreement. "Yes, we've made good distance today."

Chet reached into his vest pocket and brought out a small bottle of homemade sour mash. He took a short swig and extended the bottle for Thomas.

"Just what I need." Thomas said, taking a long gulp. "Thank you."

Chet put the bottle back inside his vest.

"I'd like to camp tonight close to water," Thomas said. "See if you can find out how long this stream carries. The place where it breaks off in the other direction is where we'll camp."

"You'd like for me to go now..."

"Keep your pistol handy," Thomas interrupted. "We need to find camp soon."

"Very well," Chet said, loosening the ropes to his horse and immediately climbing onto the saddle.

"Good. See if you can find something for dinner."

He tipped his hat at Thomas. "Yah!" Chet commanded, kicking his spurs at the horse. He disappeared almost instantly through the thick brush.

Down by the river, the others were watching as Chet rode away.

"W-wh...why is Chet going?" Megan called up to Thomas.

"He's off to find a place for us to camp for the night," Thomas said, looking at his knife, which he had just recently taken from its sleeve.

"It's no matter. Nothing for you to worry about."

"I surely wasn't worrying. I was only curious as to where he was off to. Will he be long?"

"Not too long I'd imagine."

"Well, we'll be off for a moment. Not to worry though, I have my pistol," Megan said, twirling it over her head.

"Ah, Megan; it's very important before you go," Thomas said, as if suddenly remembering, "Two fires into the air is the call for help if you find trouble."

"Oh! For Indians?" Megan asked.

"So soon Thomas," Liz asked. "We've only just started."

"Oh, and stay together," he said, loud enough for everyone to hear.

"Yes, of course." Megan declared. "We won't be too long."

Thomas watched like a mother hen as the ladies walked away, not realizing that he was holding his breath. Blue was walking up from the creek and slapped him on the back, "Relax cowboy. Everything's fine!"

"You're right," he said slightly startled. "It's only that..." He took off his hat. "Lucas will kill three times over if I don't keep his granddaughters in one piece."

"Yes, but everything will be fine. They aren't children."

"Yes, they're women!"

Blue laughed.

"Did the horses get water?" Thomas asked.

"Yes," Blue said looking down at the water.

"Good. Then we only have to wait for Chet and the women to return." Thomas said. "He should be back soon."

"I'm going to look over the wagons another time. I think the middle one is rattling too much for its own good."

"Very well." Thomas stood up to leave. "But you should rest some. The sun is out strong today."

Blue nodded his head and walked over to inspect the wagon.

Thomas quickly found a place in the shade and sat down with his back against a large tree. Blue became busy looking over the other wagons and inspecting them for cracks around the wheels. He had helped Grandpa Lucas build most of them and was familiar with their assembly.

Thomas dozed off almost immediately after sitting down, his hat tilted over his eyes. When he first sat down, he hadn't planned to sleep, but only to rest his eyes for a moment. It was difficult to avoid a nap at this time of day, though. The late afternoon sun was a sleep-causer; the strongest of men grew tired from her intensity and vigor. After a brief inspection of the wagons, Blue too fell victim to her enticing invitation. He laid down to rest.

The ladies had grown anxious from the long ride and now chatted relentlessly as they walked their way upstream. Their legs had grown tired and cramped, and they were glad to be able to stretch and rest their hands from the reins. They were searching for a more suitable place where they could attend to some personal needs, away from the men.

"Hurry Emma! I've to go badly," Megan squealed. "Why wouldn't Thomas allow us to stop for so long? 'Just drive on, just drive,' he says."

The women laughed at her impersonation of Thomas. She even acted out the hand gestures, just as Thomas did when he was giving directions or talking seriously about something.

"Gracious! I had to tell myself." Megan added. "We've been driving for such a time now and my hands have become raw from the reins."

"Megan is right Liz," Abby suddenly said. "You must speak with Thomas about this."

Emma nodded in agreement.

"Oh! This can't be good for us. It can't be healthy!" Megan said.

They giggled at Megan.

"Why am I to speak with him?" Liz said protesting.

"Well, you're the oldest of course." Megan said.

"Yes, it's true," Abby said. "If anyone were to talk with him it should be you."

"Oh fine. I will speak with him then."

Abby looked at her hands. They were red and mildly swollen. "Lizzie," she said, suddenly realizing. "Look at my hands! Are yours so swollen?"

"Good heavens, dear lady!" Liz said.

"Gracious Abby!" Emma said surprised. "Are you all right?"

"I will be fine. Does no one else have blisters from the reins?"

"Well," Liz said, "mine are faintly red, but nothing like yours."

"Yes," Megan agreed. "She's right. They are nothing like yours."

"You mustn't hold the reins so stiffly," Liz said. "Only tug when the horses misbehave."

"Yes, I know. I must have held them too tightly without realizing it."

"Let's fill our canteens down here." Liz said, watching her steps as she made her way down to the water.

The others followed her down to the creek. They were situated upriver from the men. They washed their hands and conversed for a moment, waiting on each other.

"We should get back to the wagons." Liz said, looking up at the sun. "We left awhile ago."

"Yes," Emma agreed. "Chet has probably returned by now."

The ladies finished washing and almost immediately they made their way up from the creek and followed the low-trodden down-area of grass that had led them upstream. A small line of trodden weeds and grass led the way. They had enjoyed their brief outing into the woods and felt much better after they had seen to their needs. Mostly, they had enjoyed being able to talk, something they hadn't done along the trail. It was difficult to talk then, and only important matters were worth discussing. It was scarcely worth the difficulty to converse only for the sake of conversing. It simply required too much effort and swayed the attention from the trail and the wagons in front-which, as Grandpa Lucas had said, 'wasn't a good idea.'

The women walked leisurely back to the wagons to join the men. They were in little hurry to get there. The men-hats over their eyes and sleeping-were also in no rush for them to return. They too seemed to enjoy their moment of peace.

Once the women had made their way back to the wagons, they noticed the men sleeping-each in their own shade space under a tree or wagon. John was even managing a faint snore.

*Hoonk Shuu Honk Shu*

The ladies giggled and, after a brief moment of whispering discussion, decided to wake them.

Thomas looked up, his eyes half squinted from sleep. "Wha-what is it? Has Chet returned already?"

"No," Liz said. "He hasn't returned."

"He hasn't!" Abby said, just realizing. "Should we be concerned?"

John was awakened from all of the discussion and leaned forward, listening from under the wagon. Blue too, leaned up from his tree to listen.

"I don't think so," Thomas stated. "He's only been gone for a while."

"A little while?" Megan asked somewhat sarcastically. "He's been gone for some time now. He should've returned already."

"What if…he's been bitten by a snake?" Emma added fearfully.

"Ladies please," John added from the wagon. "You're only scaring yourselves. He hasn't been gone long."

"Yes," Blue agreed. "It's nothing to worry about just yet. It won't add one cubit to your stature."

"Of course," John added from the side of the wagon. "I can only answer for myself, but there's nothing to worry about until nightfall comes."

"Aha! That's when we worry then," Megan added sarcastically.

John looked to Thomas, somewhat confused. "Yes," he finally added.

"Well, what are we to do about this," Emma demanded. "What if he's not back by nightfall?"

"What can we possibly do about it?" Thomas asked.

"Well," Emma said. "I would only hope that you wouldn't be so passive if I were the one out there and had been gone for this long."

"Emma," Liz stepped in. "Let's not worry about it just yet. We must hope that everything is fine and he will return soon."

"Can't we go look for him?" Emma pressed.

"Very well," Thomas said stepping closer to his horse. He took hold of the horse's ropes and loosed them from the tree. "I will go and search for him."

"Where will you go?" Emma questioned.

"I'll follow the river a short way," he paused, as if realizing something. "I will come back a different route."

"What are we to do here? Just wait for you!" Megan exclaimed.

Blue and John stepped closer to Thomas' horse. Luke was listening in silence, half asleep, still not sure if he were to be worried or not.

"Do you want one of us to go with you?" Luke asked.

"No, it's best that you stay here. I need for you to stay with the women and keep them calm." He said, stepping onto the horse. "I will be back soon. Do not come looking for me."

Thomas left on horseback immediately after saying this. He rushed through the thick area and disappeared at once.

Blue thought that Thomas had acted oddly. He almost suspected that Thomas knew something that he wasn't telling the others. Naturally, he kept these feelings to himself.

79

The others had become anxious from the suspicion that Chet might be in trouble. In their minds, there was a range of things that might have gone wrong, and Thomas' sudden haste only expanded these fears. Everyone's imagination began to run wild; a sort of mild hysteria seemed to come over them all. Their minds raced like stallions.

Blue was more troubled with the thought that Thomas was keeping something from him. He was almost sure of something. If Thomas didn't return as well, then he would be bound to lead the women. To what place, he wasn't sure yet. His biggest problem now was keeping everyone from going completely senseless. He felt, as the oldest man, a sense of duty, and that he ought to say something to calm them.

"Don't frown, please. It's better if we don't worry ourselves."

"Well," Megan said. "What can we do but wait for them to return?"

"I just knew something was wrong!" Emma exclaimed. "I knew he had been gone for far too long! What will we do without a scout! We can't. . ."

"Emma, please!" Liz said. "It's not certain that anything is a matter at all. Thomas will find Chet and they will return soon."

"Yes, exactly," Abby suddenly turned to Blue, as if looking for reassurance. "It may be that only he lost his way and passed by without seeing us through the brush."

"But, how could he lose his way?" Emma said. "He's only to follow the river!"

Suddenly everyone at once fell silent. Megan and Liz remained standing next to the wagons, looking at each other with questions. Emma stepped backwards and turned away from the group.

Emma looked up at the group, dropped her journal, and putting her hands to her face in tears ran to the direction of the creek.

"Oh, gracious!" Abby said. "I will go speak with her. She is tired is all."

The others watched silently as Abby went to fetch her sister.

Grandpa Lucas hadn't told any of his granddaughters, or anyone else for that matter, but he was to meet a man the following morning that was interested in leasing his logging rights to the Riverton mill. His name was Earl Babson, and he was a landowner. He already had purchased three large farms just east of Pineville, and one just north a short way. They had plenty of trees on them. He was looking for a new type of investment, and the timber business looked appealing to him. He was in his thirties-still young-and was looking for new investments.

Lucas was hopeful that he could sell the mill ahead of schedule and leave for Texas earlier than he had anticipated.

Chet and Thomas had been gone for a long time and nightfall would come soon. The sun was already low in the sky and the heat of the day had passed. It would be only a short while before the sun was down and night would arrive.

On a normal day, this would be the appropriate time for them to stop and make camp and prepare for nightfall. It was only the first day, though; and they were aware of no such routine. They weren't sure what to do, but they were worried about what news might lie ahead.

Things needed to be done, as nightfall wouldn't wait for wood that needs collecting or a place that needs further preparations before sleep. Dinner needed to be cooked. Horses needed water. There was much for them to do, but they were unmindful of this and stayed in their places, waiting under a tree or wagon for word from the men.

*How could so much happen on the first day?*

Everything had begun so perfectly. They had started early that day and made excellent time, and Thomas and Chet were in control. They had everything worked out, or so it seemed.

At their present position, they were only a day away from Pineville. They had made exceptionally good time in their first day and had journeyed farther then any of them had imagined. They could turn back now if they wanted-to safety and things they were more familiar with-and be back by late evening, the next day. They could turn around and make their way back, back to things they knew, and places that promised no risk.

Safety seemed to wait patiently in the background, hovering over them, waiting to be picked, chosen, like a ripe apple. The past, which they had seen before and were most acquainted with, lingered behind them; what lay ahead was the unknown.

Away from their hometown and on the trail, things were different. New ideas needed to be considered and previous ones needed to be discarded and rethought.

John looked up from the small log that he sat on. "Well…" he said slightly muffled. "Let's get supper on and make ready for nightfall."

Liz looked up with her hand to her mouth and was about to mutter a response, but before she could get anything out, Megan abruptly added:

"We just act like all is well and have a dinner party?"

"What are we to eat then? We've nothing."

"I hardly think that is true," Megan said. "We have plenty of food to eat."

"Yes," Abby jumped in. "It's only the first day. We've plenty to eat. Besides," she said seriously. "I would suspect that we should have things in order when Chet and Thomas return. It's almost sunset and they will probably be back soon."

"I'd like to cook something up very much indeed," Blue added. "But, we should prepare for nightfall. It will be dark soon."

John stood up quickly and placed his hat over his head. "Blue and I will tend to the horses and wagons. Luke, help the ladies collect wood for a fire."

Luke nodded his head and immediately started to search for wood.

With a newfound sense of haste, the group worked quickly, preparing for nightfall. The sky was still bright, but growing dimmer by the moment. It had acquired that fleeting look it often gets just before sunset, which indicates its eventual end is in prospect. The group moved with urgency.

# Chapter 12
## The Leaders

**W**ADING THROUGH THE THICK BRUSH, Thomas looked for signs that Chet might have left behind. Since he was not trying to hide his tracks, he should be easy to follow. Chet had not been gone long, but Thomas had a bad feeling.

The forest was heavy with underbrush. It was like a deep ocean that someone could fall into and disappear.

Thomas looked ahead into a small clearing. He could not believe his eyes as he looked up. Standing before him was Chet's painted pony, rider-less. The calm horse stood there, munching on a green bush, with one bridle rein dragging the rocky water's edge.

The horse looked up, chewing, and shook his head, as if to say hello. He whinnied at Thomas and quickly returned to his supper. Thomas rode up close, swung one leg over his mare and slid down. He patted the spotted pony and checked for signs that would tell him how Chet might have evacuated his mount. The pony was well and he found no blood from the horse or the rider. The saddlebag and bedroll were intact and showed no signs from injury. Everything was as safe and normal as a church picnic.

Thomas scouted the area for a trail or clue of where Chet could be. His eyes skimmed the water. As Thomas was walking to the far edge of the clearing he heard something.

It was getting dusky dark now and difficult to see the shadows.

There lay Chet, his head by the edge of a sharp rock. Dried blood was on his head at the hairline and on the rock near Chet's head.

"Chet," Thomas said softly. "What happened! You all right?"

Chet moaned again and half-opened his eyes for a second.

"I knew that," Chet struggled to say each word, his head pounding, "you would come. The women made you."

Thomas cleaned up the cut and washed the blood away with cool water. They were close to the big creek that they had been following earlier. He gave Chet a small drink of water from his canteen. The head injury didn't appear to be very serious, but Thomas wrapped his head with a long rag and pulled it tight.

Thomas tethered the horses to a tree line and unsaddled them for the night.

"Your head isn't bleeding very badly, but it's too dark to ride back tonight. We will have to camp here until morning," said Thomas.

The thick forest surrounded them on all sides so that there was no large area to make a camp. Thomas cleared the leaf-strewn ground for their bedrolls and quickly built a small fire.

Thomas was baffled as to what might have happened to Chet and his pony. It seemed unusual to him because Chet was an excellent rider and worked well with his horse; he had trained her himself. Most all Texas cowboys took great pride in their horses; the degree to which each horse could read the mind of the rider was a great consideration. Chet had spent a great amount of time training his mount exactly as he

86

had wanted. It seemed odd to Thomas that this could have happened as it did.

Thomas ran his hand down the leg of the filly again and lifted her foot. What had made him fall?

Thomas tried to make Chet more comfortable for the night. Each time he tried to move him he moaned in pain. He went over each bone to see if any were broken. All seemed to be well. Just one nasty cut on the head. He wished he had some needle and thread, which was back at the camp. Emma always had her quilt bag close by. She kept it around her waist looking for an idle moment to put a nine-patch block together.

Now with his head resting on his own saddle, his eyes begin to drift asleep. Slight but heavy footsteps padded close to the clearing. He opened one eye and both ears. He couldn't see anything. The horses sensed danger. They began to toss their manes and become nervous.

Thomas slowly moved his hand to the side of his leg where his gun was strapped. He pulled it from its holster.

He waited, but heard nothing. The horses settled slightly, but Thomas felt as though something or someone was watching them. He did not know how or why Chet was thrown from his saddle but something was amiss.

A few moments passed, Thomas sat up and stirred the fire. He placed more wood on the burning coals. He intended to keep the fire up high tonight. Something was out there watching. He looked over to Chet. He was sleeping.

Several miles back at the wagon camp, the night had become eerie.

Luke's dog, Bear, was sitting silently around the campfire next to his master. John and Blue talked about the turn of events from the day and considered their options for in the morning.

Bear had his head on his front paws, which were crossed. His eyes moved to each man as they talked. Suddenly, the dog's nostrils flared as he picked up an unusual smell. His nose twitched, trying to get more of the smell. Immediately, the dog rose and hastily flounced into the darkness.

"What is it boy?" Lucas asked, looking through the under carriage of the wagons and wheels. He tried to adjust his eyes to the blackness of the night after staring at the campfire for so long.

Lucas could see his dog now; he was up on all fours and alert on something. He let out a low growl, just to let the adversary know that he meant business. His throat puffed and his black lips curled up, exposing his black gums and long pointed teeth. The deep growl continued and grew more intense. He now had the attention of Blue and John, with guns in hand.

"Are all the women in the wagons?" Blue directed to no one in particular.

"Yes." Luke answered still searching the darkness.

"What is it?" He asked.

"I don't know." Blue said "But the back of my neck is crawling."

"I don't like it at all." John said quietly, his finger on the trigger of his revolver.

"What was that! Did you hear that?" Luke looked to his friends.

"No, what'd you hear?" Blue asked.

Bear's gaze never left the small gap in the trees. He prowled toward it, more confident now that the others had arrived. He let out a fierce bark that Lucas didn't know his dog could make.

Suddenly, a white form emerged. Megan was in her nightgown, panting and looking around frantically, her face white like a ghost.

"Good God Megan! What are you doing out there?" Blue asked irritated and relieved. His gun went down. "Are you alone?"

John let out a breath and bent over to his knees. Bear was now at the opening Megan had flown through, his throat still rumbling.

"Come here boy." Luke pressed.

Bear didn't move.

"What was that? Did you see it?" She panted, trying to catch her breath.

"We didn't see anything. We only heard it." Blue said.

"Well, what did you see?" John asked impatiently.

"Megan you know not to go out alone. Did you even tell anyone?" Blue asked.

She ignored his correction.

"It was big with glowing eyes. It moved so quickly. Did you hear it? I haven't a clue what it was, but it could have gotten me! It's still out there." Megan cried.

"Aunt Megan, what do you think it is?" Luke asked.

"I'm going to the wagon." Megan withdrew with quick steps.

The men were left standing there, looking to the dark opening in the woods where Bear was guarding.

# Chapter 13
## A Spell of Bad Luck

CHET RAISED ONE ARM UP to his head injury. He began to remember the previous day and how he had fallen from his horse. His eyes worked to open. His muscles felt stiff and difficult to move, his legs like watered-down logs.

Am I alive or dead?

If he were dead, surely his head would not hurt so badly. He must be alive. He could hear water and a noise that sounded like movement.

"Goo-morning cowboy, you still with me?" Thomas asked.

Chet recognized Thomas' voice and tried to open his eyes again.

"What happened?" Chet asked.

"I was hoping you would give me the details." Thomas said, amused at Chet's confusion.

"Where's my pony? Is my girl fine?" He asked Thomas.

Thomas poured coffee and walked over to his friend.

"She is fine. I checked her over last night and this morning, looking for a few answers. I tried to get her to tell me what happened." Thomas smiled. "She wouldn't talk."

He took the coffee Thomas offered and rested on one elbow. It was hot, but not too good. He forgot how bad the coffee was that Thomas always brewed.

Thomas watched Chet; he didn't look badly wounded.

"And I think you're fine too. Do you think you can ride today?"

"I think so, how deep is the cut?"

The cut on his head was still oozing and his hair was matted together with blood at his hairline.

"We need to get you to Miss Emma's sewing bag. She can put in a real neat stitch, maybe it won't scar." Thomas looked at the open gash. "After breakfast, I figure I will ride back to the camp and alert the others to where you are. We can bring the wagons through this way and settle you back on one until you're keen to ride."

Chet managed a small nod and carefully sipped his coffee.

"I should make return with the wagons late morning."

Chet nodded again. "That should be just fine," he managed.

Thomas looked to Chet. "So what made a cowboy like you get thrown from his best filly?"

"Well," Chet cleared his throat and prepared himself to speak; he sat up. "We were riding along this beautiful creek, when she got spooked for no reason that I could tell. We got to this clearing and we were trapped with only one way out. I heard a growl which appeared to be rather close." Chet grew more excited as he spoke. "Immediately!" He clapped his hands together. "I looked up and could see a huge black, panther about to lunge at us. Just then, Tessie bolted!" Chet stopped and thought for a moment. "And that was the last thing I remember. I thought we were both sure to be supper!"

"A panther?" Thomas questioned.

"Yes, sir. I know it was."

"You didn't have any idea that this cat was after you? I've seen a few before but they usually aren't so aggressive.

"Yah." Chet answered. "I hadn't a clue that anything was around. Tessie did not even have much warning. Usually she can smell danger and warn me that something is around."

"How do you reckon Tessie got away?"

"She must have fought and kicked her way out of the clearing and then ran for her life. The big cat must have tired and missed out on both of us."

They both sipped their coffee.

"Where did you find her?" Chet asked.

"Not too far from you right now. She was all lathered up. I could tell she had been run hard; but, she was calm when I rode close up on her."

Chet was reminded by the pounding in his head that he was thrown and still hurt. He lay back to rest his head on the saddle and closed his eyes. His head was pounding. "Ride on back to camp. I will be fine here."

Thomas unloosed his mare from the lanky oak tree, which all night he had fought with for sleeping space. He checked his saddle and prepared to ride back to camp. He was not completely sure that Chet was well enough to ride. He knew that he needed to rest more and he would have time before the wagons made their way back. Hopefully, he would be back to himself the next day.

"Rest a bit more. I will be back with the wagons well before noon."

At breakfast and at the campfire, Megan told her story to Liz, Abby, and Emma.

"Tell us." Emma asked.

93

"What it was exactly," Megan said, "I'm not sure; but it was big, dark and quick as lightning. That was the part that was so strange and frightening to me. It would have easily torn me to pieces, provided I didn't run like the devil to get back to camp!" She shook when she went over it again.

"Megan, I am upset with your judgment. You should never go out alone like that, and you did not even tell any of us!" Liz scolded her sister.

"I know, but I always have to go one more time and I didn't want to disturb anyone. All of you were already asleep."

"It is only the second day and we've already lost Thomas and Chet; and you go out last night all by yourself? How could you do something like that? I just don't understand. What if you didn't come back? And then, what would we do this morning with three people missing? We already don't know what to do now!"

Megan didn't say anything.

"Well…" Liz demanded an explanation.

"I'm sorry Liz. You're right." Megan lowered her head. "I shouldn't have done that."

Blue approached the ladies from his wagon, pulling up his pants along the way. He managed a groggy, "Goo-morning," to the group of women.

"Good morning," they said flatly.

He rinsed a tin cup and prepared to make coffee.

"Where is Luke?" Liz directed to Blue.

"Sleeping still."

Liz stood seriously and put her hands on her hips, as if to say something. "What should we do this morning? Do we stay here and continue to wait or do we go search for them?"

Blue looked up, as though not yet ready to answer such a question.

"I don't think we ought to search for them." Abby said.

"Yes, me either." Emma agreed.

"Yes," Blue said from his cup. "I don't think that would be wise either. We stay here and wait. That's all we can do. If they come back and we're not here, then they will be lost."

Just then, over the hill that blocked their campsite from the river, the group could see someone approaching on horseback.

"Who is it?" Emma asked

"Is it Chet?" asked Abby.

"No," Liz said. "It's Thomas!"

The group hastily approached the swift rider. Thomas pulled back on the reins and the horse came to an abrupt stop. "Everything's fine," he said immediately, slightly out of breath. "Chet is all right. He fell from his horse and injured his head, but he's going to be just fine."

"Oh! Thank God!" Liz exclaimed. "Thank God!"

"What happened," Abby questioned. "He fell from his horse?"

"Yes, his horse got spooked and threw him. He hit his head and was knocked out entirely. I approached him just as he was coming to. It was too dark for us to ride back to camp."

"What spooked his horse?" Megan asked.

"He wasn't sure."

"Well, where is Chet now?"

"We will pack and prepare to leave. He is waiting for us by the creek."

"Gracious Thomas," Liz said pensively. "We were worried so. We didn't know what we would do this morning."

"Yes," said Emma. "Thank God everything is well."

"Well, everything is fine," said Thomas.

"Thank God."

"I feel so foolish now," Abby said, "to think how we overreacted yesterday."

"Yes." Megan said.

"But," Abby continued, "We weren't prepared for a matter as that, and so soon on the trail."

"Yes," Liz agreed. "It just happened too soon, but thank God everything is fine."

"Yes." Abby nodded.

"Well," said Thomas, "Let's pack up. Chet's a-waiting."

To the south, the sky was growing dark and green.

# Chapter 14
## The Split

**T**HE WAGONS WERE SLOW TO GET STARTED. Eight teams and wagons to get hitched-up took awhile to make ready. Megan twisted her hand in one of the riggings, trying to help John with her team. Finally, they were ready to roll out of their camp. Thomas' wagon and team were hooked together with Blue's. Thomas was in the lead wagon; he had decided they would travel in a single wagon row because of the narrowness along the small river. They followed along the creek until it forked south.

Liz thought it looked like a noonday sun as she looked out from her bonnet. They had traveled what seemed to be a long enough distance. Chet would be close by. To the southwest, all that could be seen was darkness and fast-moving rain clouds; the sun would be blocked soon.

Thomas slowed the lead wagon to an abrupt halt and jumped down. He unloosed his horse and walked back to the others who were stretching their arms.

"Thomas," Blue called out, "Those clouds are moving fast."

Thomas took off his hat and looked up to the dark clouds. "Where did those come from?"

"I was watching them as we rode." Blue said. "I thought they would move north, away from us."

"Keep everyone in their wagons. Chet is down through the brush a few leagues; I will be back with him."

"Well fine, but what about those clouds? They're green!"

"Only a little rain. I will be back!"

Thomas rode his horse down a steep hill and through the brush. The trees were thicker as he got closer to the creek. Before he reached the bottom of the hill, he could already fill raindrops on his neck. His horse shivered from an unexpected south wind.

"Whew! That's cold Bootsie!" His horse grunted. "Keep going, we're almost there."

Bootsie plowed her way through the thick bushes. Small branches scraped across Thomas' face, he tried to shield himself with his arm. A narrow area of smooth stones and rocks bordered the skinny river and made it less thick with growth. Just as Thomas reached this area, he could see Chet's horse and bag.

"Chet," he called out from atop his horse.

He could see Chet eating a dried piece of meat, seated on a fallen tree. "Chet, we got to get going! A storm is coming in."

Chet looked up, happy to see his friend. The long rag, which he had worn across his head, was now in his back pocket.

"How do you feel?" asked Thomas.

"I can ride."

Chet hurried to place his cup and food into Tessie's saddlebag. He hastily hopped on.

Meanwhile, back at the wagons, the wind was blowing fiercely. The flaps on Liz's bonnet were pressed against her face. A gust of wind caught her attention and compelled her to look up. The huge dark storm was already upon them. She could tell that it would soon be raining harder than it already was.

Over the day before, and that morning, the heat had built up quickly. Liz was surprised at herself; she was normally more alert to the weather. As a young child, she had been taught how to read the weather and how to distinguish a severe storm from a mere rainstorm. Liz, in turn, had schooled Luke on the weather.

Liz scolded herself; for she always worked hard to be prepared for such circumstances, and it was frustrating to her that she was caught off guard. Liz looked back to the group.

*Maybe we should take cover.*

Next to Blue's wagon-in the back of the line-the branches of two dead trees hung over the horses. A strong flurry of wind blew across the tree's limbs. Suddenly, the base of the tree's limbs-where it connected with the rest of the trunk-cracked off. The large dead limbs came crashing to the ground in one swift movement, yet almost in slow motion. The limbs fell right next to Blue's team of horses. Just as they cracked to the ground, Blue's side horse got spooked from the commotion and immediately began to run. Blue was still onboard; he tried to gain control over his horses, but couldn't.

As the horses began to sprint to safety, the back wheel clipped the side of Lucas' wagon, sparking a great disorder with all of the horses. Before anyone knew it, each wagon and all the teams of horses were sprinting away. The rain began to pelt stronger, faster and faster. All of the drivers were still onboard, and none could gain control; in only a few anomalous moments, they had quickly become passengers.

99

The temperature had dropped dramatically and the sky had turned a sickly pond green. The storm was in full-force now with the sky pumped full of electrical power. It was windy and cold. Thomas did not like their location under a group of trees but he had no choice. He also had no choice but to wait again. Blue was right, this was a wicked storm. Hail the size of sand-hill plums began to beat the leaves off of the trees around them. Thunder cracked above them and a bolt of lighting split a huge pecan tree. A branch fell, cracking a little too close to where they waited. Thomas' horse reared up pulling the reins from his master and disappeared in the dark depressed storm.

Thomas was beginning to think that a bad luck spell had been placed upon him.

The rumble of the storm continued to drop massive amounts rain all night long. Thomas and Chet had found an area under some thick trees to stay as dry as possible. The cover was insufficient and they were already cold and wet to the core. Chet hated that his boots were soaked. Thomas kept a close eye on the creek. He did not want to be caught in a flash flood.

"Thomas? Do you think any of the big paw prints we had found will still be around in the morning?"

"No," he answered

"I don't see how in this storm. They were the biggest I have ever seen. It would have to be a large cat, what the Indians call Puma. They pull their claws in when they walk. Dogs and coyotes even bobcats leave a claw mark when they walk. These panthers can get pretty big. I once saw four-inch pad tracks on a black one. It stalked us for two days over in east Texas. Killed one of our horses just for sport, didn't take one bite from him. It was evil, just plain evil."

Thomas looked over to Chet, water streaming off the brim of his cowboy hat and on to his poncho.

"What else do you know about these black panthers?"

"Puma cats have front paws that are larger than the back. When they walk, their back paws step into the print of the front one, causing overlap of the paw prints. They walk clean straight lines. Their prints are distinct with three lobes at the heel of the paw print or pad and two at the top, with four toes. Those tracks we saw today are puma prints. It has to be a black panther and the size is the biggest I have ever seen or heard of. That's what spooked Tessie, I'm sure of it. I scouted with an old Indian. He told of a legend about a black puma. It was an evil spirit to his people. It would stalk his people and bring bad luck. As long as it prowled about, destruction was close at hand."

Thomas wasn't sure he believed in evil spirits or legends with curses, but luck didn't seem to be on his side. This was a day from hell and he was already inclined for it to be over.

Thunder boomed overhead. The rain slowed to a heavy drizzle. He glanced toward the stream once more. It was rising and moving more quickly but it was nothing to be concerned over. Where his horse had run to, was his greatest concern; and, whether or not she was safe from the puma.

"Where do you reckon the women are?" Chet asked.

"I hope they are just up the hill a short way. There were plenty of trees I saw, for them to take cover."

"I'm sure they're fine. There's no sense in us walking up that muddy hill with it raining like this."

"Well, we know which way to head in the morning after I find my mare. I hope they had the teams tied up good in all of this thunder. If we get an early start we can be there before they have time to be

anxious. Hopefully, our bad luck was washed away in this weather."
Thomas said-who, now more secure with his decision, decided to
catch a wink or two until the storm passed and they could meet up
with the wagons.

Lightning flashed across the dark sky, revealing a snaking twister
that reached towards the ground and nearly touched. Liz could see the
lanky tornado over the trees; it would be on the ground soon.

"Twister!" Liz called to the frantic group that was now gaining
control of their battered wagons. "Take cover!" She said again. "It's
coming our way! We need to find a low spot, get to a shelter!"

Blue pointed to a ravine that was only a short ways from where
they were. The teams of horses seemed as eager as the drivers to find
safety; they moved without prompting.

Liz was surprised at how easy it had been to get the wagons to the
ravine. They had all made it there quickly. The horses were jittery over
the hailstones that now began to bounce from their targets. They had
nothing to tie the teams to and they would surely spook and run
again. They would have to hold two sets of teams. Liz was concerned
for Luke, who was standing away from the shelter and holding his
team, but there was no choice in the matter. John, Blue, Luke and Liz
each did their best to keep two teams calm during the worst of it. Hail
pounded Liz across the shoulders as she tried to protect herself next
to the animals and hold the reins to keep them calm. Her bonnet was
up, but what was the use. She was soaked to the skin and shivering.
She nestled in closer to the horse and tucked her head under the soft
velvet jaw of its neck. She wondered who was comforting whom. The
wind whipped her dress around her legs and embraced her. She
looked out to see how Luke was doing; the wind whipped her bonnet
back and a hailstone hit her on the mouth. Her lip was cold-numb and

she could taste blood. Liz hung her head down under the protection of her horse; huge sobs escaped from her.

"Where are you, Caleb? We need you. Why did you leave us?" Liz cried. The rain mixed with her tears. She could not keep the feeling away that came in with the storm, a grave feeling of hopelessness. The rain that hit her face brought back the memory of the Riverton Mill and the day she became the widow of Caleb Bromont. Such circumstances as these made her think of the fabric-chain which she had placed in Caleb's Irish Quilt; it had been for good luck. At times like these, she felt that she needed some of it.

*Where is my chain of promise?*

Liz looked over again to Luke. He was becoming a man just like Grandpa said. The storm was still threatening and his two teams were doing well as the others were also. The hail had now passed and hopefully the threat of the twister too. Liz looked around to see if she could tell where they were. The teams had run quite a distance; and now, as they sat under the cold, damp trees, it was beginning to grow dark.

"Liz," Abby called. "Hurry, come inside. The thunder is almost gone now, the horses will be fine."

Abby had the strings untied from the wagon cover and was holding them tightly as the wind whipped about. She would not lose control of them and let the wind or rain inside her-almost-dry abode.

Liz gave a word of encouragement to the animals and pulled her black boots from the mud and streams of water that flooded past her ankles. Her dress was saturated and had lost all its absorbing power; the water passed right by her hemline. She was bone-tired and beat as she waded her way to Abby, her dress weighing more than she did. She nearly missed the wooden ledge on the wagon bed. As she was climbing up to comfort, her heel caught the edge of her skirt and ripped it at the waist. Her hand slipped off the top edge of the wagon and she fell hitting her check bone on the wooden sideboard.

*Now what else? What else?*

Abby heard the whack of Liz's face against the wagon.

"Oh my, Liz! Are you hurt?" Abby said, pensively.

Liz was now in the wagon, setting in a state of exhaustion with mud, blood and tears burning over her cut swollen face. Abby, seeing her distress, quickly went to work.

"Megan and Emma are in the wagon over there." She motioned to the back corner of her wagon as she was caring for her cut cheek and pulling out some dry things for her cousin. She turned around to grab the wagon cover cords and peeked out. She pulled them tight and dropped the big flap from the top. She pulled another string around a toggle nailed to the wagon's side.

"Luke just climbed up in his wagon and the men are headed to theirs. Hopefully the worst is over. Oh Liz, you are drenched and bleeding. I hope you don't catch your death of a cold. Hurry and dry off."

Liz pulled what was left of her dress from her body and put the small cloth around her hair. As she swept her hair up in the flour sack, Abby saw her battered shoulder where the hailstones had bruised her skin. Liz jumped as the cotton sack touched her tender shoulders.

"I don't know which is worse. I feel beat inside and out." Liz sighed. "Luke's in his wagon?"

"Yes."

"I hope he has his pinwheel quilt where he can use it."

Liz had quilted Luke's quilt with wool batting from Mrs. Dongreen's flock of sheep. Liz thought she made the best wool batting; she could afford one length a year.

"It will help keep Luke dry. It is the best for humid climates, though. Oh…I must be delirious rambling on like this dear Abby." Liz popped her head into the surprisingly dry and welcome nightgown.

The rain continued to come down in sheets all night long. Liz was so exhausted that, again, she did not remember her head hitting her pillow. She pulled Abby's soft worn quilt up to her battered shoulder and snuggled into its comfort and warmth. As she drifted off to sleep she thought surely that Caleb would arrive in the morning and take them safely to their new home in the west. Somewhere in her foggy thought came the realization that Caleb would never be home. She was on her own.

The sun would be up in an hour and the rain was now falling like a gentle shower. The ravine they had camped in was a flood zone for this type of gully washers. The water had begun to rise in the night as the storm raged on. A lapping of water had been washing away at the topsoil around the wheels of Blues wagon all night long. Finally, the wagon began to groan and shift as the ground gave way beneath. This activity woke Blue up and he sprang to the wagon seat.

"John! John!" Blue cried." Wake up! Get them all up! Hurry, flash flood!"

Blue was grabbing the reins of his team and releasing the brake to pull against the water. His team sprang into action and started to pull the wagon up to higher ground. The women awoke and clambered about to reach their own wagons without touching the rain-soaked ground.

For several minutes, driver and team worked hard pulling the wagons from the clay ruts. Finally, Liz realized all the wagons but one were on higher ground. The wagon Thomas was driving had no driver to direct it to safety. It was being pulled closer to the open rushing water current. The horses pulling against it could barely keep it from being swept away. It had attached one of its wheels to a large rock and tree stump. They would have to act fast in order to keep the team and wagon from being lost, and, all of their contents.

Liz scampered across a branch that had fallen and created a bridge. It would take her to the rock where she could jump into the drifted wagon seat.

"John! Blue!" She called. "Hurry to the wheel. As soon as I grab the reins, break the branch and release the wheel."

There was no time to tell her to let it go. They had to help her.

Blue held onto the wagon as he worked his way around to the tree branch, which had lodged its way inside the spokes.

"Ready." Liz called out and started to encourage the horses to pull with all their might. Four horses pulled, two men pushed, four on dry land prayed.

Suddenly, with a mighty push, the wagon was free and the horses were on dry land. John and Blue held on to the back of the wagon until they could walk and not be in danger of the rushing waters grabbing their ankles.

"Well, good morning everyone." John said, good heartedly. "I see we are off to a good start already."

They laughed.

"We won't have to wash up for breakfast," John added with a chuckle.

Blue looked at himself dripping in muddy water and suddenly noticed his torn shirt.

"Miss Liz what do you have in that wagon. It is as heavy as gold bricks. What did Thomas pack?"

Liz was shocked over the gold brick statement. The reason she saved the wagon, in fact, was because it was filled with her grandfather's gold; information that, at the instructions of Grandpa Lucas, was only for Thomas and herself. Luckily, it had been saved from disaster.

As John walked away to prepare the wagons, he placed his arm around Luke, who was standing in the same place he had been through the entire ordeal and still unable to believe what he had just witnessed.

"That is one special lady, that mother of yours. I was feeling pain from those hailstones last night and was ready to give up when I looked around and saw her out there with the men. Soaked and beat up but never giving up. Now she pulls a wagon from a watery grave in her nightgown. Even with a shiner and a split lip. If Thomas doesn't hurry back, I might have to ask her to marry me!" John slapped Luke on the back and withdrew to his wagon. "Even pulled a wagon from a flash flood in her night dress." He mumbled to himself shaking his head in disbelief.

Luke looked over to his mother climbing down from the rescued wagon in the soft predawn light. His grandfather respected Thomas and he was always around; but he was always around when his dad was here too. He would have to consider this awhile. He liked John just fine, but simply couldn't see him with his mother and had never thought of it.

They had a lot to do before they would be ready to leave. The teams needed to be unharnessed and rubbed down. The horses had worn wet-riggings all night. The wagons would need to be checked for wear, or any damage they had suffered at the hands of the wild horses. Each wagon needed to be dried out correctly. The day before, Megan had hurt her hand helping Blue hitch her wagon. Liz spent some time feeding the chickens. She was surprised to find a couple of eggs waiting for her, both unbroken. Luke made sure his special quilt was dry and folded in his wagon. Bear had done well in the storm and was excited to get out and run. Luke decided that he would let him run with the wagons once they left. Soon, they would be ready to continue on the trail.

Liz had thought about where they were and what to do to find Thomas and Chet. She was sure that if they continued on in their direction, that Thomas and Chet would eventually meet up with them.

When all was ready Liz stood before the group and informed them of the plan. Liz explained that both Thomas and Chet were sure to catch up with them, but that they should make haste, considering that all that day they had traveled virtually no distance at all. Everyone seemed to be in agreement.

"We follow the sun west." Blue informed her and they started the third day with the worst sleep yet.

It took all day for Chet and Thomas to locate Bootsie. They eventually headed back to the big group of trees where they had last been all together. They searched for signs that might tell them where the group was. They couldn't find anything. The wagons were not where they had left them and there was so much mud that they couldn't make out any tracks. The storm had washed away any tracks that might have been useful. The campsite was empty.

"I think we should ride southwest and see if we can pick up a trail." Thomas said from his tall horse. "I don't believe they would have headed back to Lecompte."

Chet nodded.

"Let's spread out within shotgun range and search for tracks."

Thomas had thought about the group during the storm, and how they had fared. He had no idea how bad it had been or where they were. As he made his way up a steep hill, he could see where a small twister had gone through one area, leaving a clearing where trees had once stood. The trees were pulled up like small weeds in a garden. The loose ground was plowed up like gunfire.

Thomas and Chet searched all day, but couldn't find any sign of the group, neither tracks nor hoof prints.

# Chapter 15
## The Journal

**L**IZ DECIDED IT WAS AN EXCELLENT TIME TO START writing in her little journal that Abby had given them. She thought it would be good to write the daily events and to record her frustrations and opinions. Not that anyone would ever care, but that it would be beneficial for her. She wanted to put the first three days into words if she could, considering their tremendous hardships they had encountered. Her grandchildren would never believe the escapades that she and the others had experienced. Her hand went to her cheek bone and touched her wound; she picked up her little pencil and began to write. She wrote neatly the headline:

*May 1856, Elizabeth Bromont's Journey to Fort Worth, Texas*

Liz started by giving the accounts of the first two days. When she came to the third day, she began to write the following:

*We have made a small stopover; it is lovely thus far. The ground is fresh from the rain. The scenery appears to be the same as grandfather's beloved Riverton home. The trees and wildflowers are sweet and untouched. We are faring better as the day has gone along. Luke and his dog, Bear, are good help and they are enjoying the trip, even with the mishaps. For him, I suppose it adds to such an adventure. Bear cornered a rabbit for supper and our group is happy to have meat that is fresh. It will be a lovely treat. With all that we have encountered, our meals have lacked that which we are accustomed to.*

*This afternoon, the sky clouded up again, reminding us all of the days before when the fierce rain nearly took our wagon and team of horses. I prayed and therein it passed by. Megan is excited that her prized treadle machine weathered the storm sans any undoings. I, too, am excited we've made it thus far, and, for the most part, in one piece. Megan remains confident and contented about life, including every detail of it. Though, I wish Emma could consider such outlooks. Megan is elated even to cook our rabbit stew for the night. She also has made plans to cook biscuits, a lovely treat on such a journey. Megan has mentioned that, on her account, we should not withhold any consideration we might have to travel all the way to California. For me though, if I can make it to Texas, I suppose I will never leave.*

*Day four:*
*I consider us to be faring and managing well. To sleep on the ground is our greatest discomfort. Though, we are dry and that continues to be a great luxury. We, too, are not cramped in wagons.*

Throughout the day's travel, we become very weary from the intense turbulence of the wagon's ride; and, at night, we are contented only to be still, for the wagons shake us beyond belief. Blue's team of oxen smell so bad in the day's heat. After today, we've agreed that it would be best for him to drive at the rear of the train from here on out.

At night, we have been required to cook over an open fire. It is different in many ways, though I am already growing more accustomed to it. It is amazing how such tasks can quickly become routine.

I consider it a peculiarity the way in which the men have allowed me to be leader of the group, and be the manager of even the smallest considerations. Many times and throughout the day, I have considered our direction west and have rightly hoped that we are going the correct angle, south and west. Thomas and Chet have now been gone two complete days. I do not allow myself or the others to dwell on this.

Blue and John are faring well with the repairs that our wagons might require. They, too, are trying to keep us safe. Each evening when we make camp, Blue goes to each wagon and checks it over for any damages that might have been made throughout the day. With his hands, he pushes and pulls on all facets of the wagon, making certain that every inch is favorable. They rarely speak to us women. Methinks that they feel a certain responsibility to Grandpa Lucas; and, perchance, they are already concerned about his opinion of the trouble we've encountered. Blue does well, rigging the harnesses so that each of us women can handle the wagons. Blue has taken both of the oxen teams and follows behind us as we make our way. Of course, he eventually catches up to us after we stop for camp each evening. I have decided to push long each day. The sooner that we can reach the edge of Texas, the sooner we will meet with the Rangers. John, too, takes care of the teams well. One harness is rubbing badly and we've had to make some salve from the root of a stickery bush. I *decided to try it on the injuries to my face. It helped the soreness and seems to be healing faster, though it stains my face purple so that the others laughed at me.*

*John and Blue have brought whiskey. He put some in my coffee and it helps me to sleep better; I was not as sore and tender the next day.*

*Day five:*

*The weather has been hot. Now and then, we get a cloud which gives us a short spell of relief, but it seems to make the air more thick. I want nothing more than to find a place where we could take a swim and rest an afternoon. Our clothes are so damp that they stick to us. I would like to change clothes, but don't want to until we find a place to rest and bathe. I am still wearing my torn dress from the storm. I did a quick repair on the waist. I know that I must look a fright with my injuries and my dress torn. Megan said she would fix it better than new for me. She has been so worried over the trouble I had. I am glad that we had no broken bones. Blue said if it would rain we could all take a shower. Megan and Emma keep us on our toes, the rascals. We are all sore from the shaking of the wagons and the team handling. Though I haven't looked at the condition of our freight, I am glad that we had the sawdust for packing. I will put a little of John's whiskey in all of our coffee tonight. We all need to sleep well at least once this week.*

*Day six:*

*About mid-morning, we found the perfect place to bathe and take a short swim. I halted the wagons and told the team that this ought to be our day of repair and rest. They all agreed. Camp was made after only a few hours of travel time. We did repairs on the wagons, and we washed clothes and repaired them as well. The rest and cleanliness was good for our souls. After supper Blue and John pulled out some instruments and we enjoyed some music and sang our*

favorite hymns. We even had a dance or two, though I know many forbid it. We all pulled out our quilting and stitched during the late afternoon and before supper. Emma cheered up a great deal after we sewed. I asked her if she had tried to stitch in her wagon as we traveled. She said that she had and that it hurt too much. She showed me her sore fingers. She laughed and said that it didn't work on the stage either. It was a wonderful day. Megan said that it was starting to look different as we passed through uncharted land, which we had never before seen. As I went to the wagon to sleep tonight, I asked John what he thought about Thomas and Chet still missing. He reassured me that they would be along soon and not to worry. I think what he says is true.

Day seven:

I was surprised this morning as we came upon Fort Polk. We stopped and got a few supplies and had a nice visit with some of the officer's wives. They prepared a magnificent lunch for us; it did our souls well to have such food and hospitality. We surely were not ready to go when the Captain gave the call to load up. All of us had made friends quickly, even Luke and Bear. The young troops were interested in our unusual group and quickly saddled up to escort us to the border where our Rangers are supposed to be waiting. They said that we ought to be there by evening. I was upset when I learned we had angled south too far and now would have to go north to our location in Texas. We have lost time by our troubles and by losing our direction. The Lieutenant assured me that the storm had disrupted the path we were to be on and we would have had to come south anyway. Truth? I'm not sure of it, but it made me feel better. I also decided that Thomas and Chet are fine and that they must be worried sick over us, and wondering where we are. I hope they have not been back to grandfather, I would hate for him to worry so over us when we are well. It was a good thing also that we cleaned up yesterday.

We would have died for all to see us in such disarray as we were. Captain Sewell was concerned over my injuries and had the doctor of the fort take a look at my head scrape. He scolded me and said a lady had no business doing this. I'm not sure what he thought "this" was or that I enjoyed it. He said to keep putting the salve on, and that which we made for the horses; even though it turns one's skin purple. Captain Sewell also advised us on the route to take north after we cross over the line and he said he would put word out to Thomas and Chet as to our whereabouts. He said the Indians have been quiet lately, but that we will go through a certain territory where we should stay most alerted. Mrs. Sewell had a new baby girl that we all fell in love with. I think all of us were thinking about our own mothering feelings and wondering if we would have our own in the future. I don't know why Caleb and I never had more. Luke came so quickly I assumed I would have plenty. Abby and Megan certainly are old enough to have a houseful of their own by now. It is, in fact, quite unusual for all of us to be single and Luke the only child. I never thought of it in such a way until just recently. We made the Texas line by dark and the army made camp with us. They drew us a map and gave us the landmarks for which we should stand watch as we move farther west.

Day eight:

This morning it was rather difficult to see the troops ride away. I slept well in light of not having one of John's special coffee mixtures; my body feels well and my injuries are all but healed. Megan always has admirers, and certainly she is pleasant to them; she never seems to have an interest in anyone, though.

As we continue, we are to go along the Angelina River and the forest. As I saw all of the lumber from the trees, I began to wonder if Grandpa ought to leave the lumbering business. It seems like ages since we were back home. I haven't the time or the energy to worry over the things as I did in Lecompte.

Captain Sewell's wife showed us a number of her patterns, and I have just now realized that I forgot to write them down. She had many beautiful quilts, which we all loved, my favorite being a star, of course, and with a blue center and points. It had a small burst of triangles around it. It will be the first one I make after I settle in my new home. As always, we traded some cloth with her. She had some of the blue from the star, and, being the lady that she is, simply gave it to me. I promised to inform her on my progress and she wished me luck; we all thanked her. She had more quilts than I had ever before seen, almost all of which were stacked and neatly folded. She rarely uses many of them. I suppose that she has a lot of empty time on her hands. Another, which I liked a great deal, was one that had a wreath with points. It was very unusual in its design. Each circle had a bluish hue to it. It appears to be nothing more than what I refer to as an organized scrap quilt. It seems difficult to make. Upon curiosity, I counted over seventy pieces in each block. It had many curved pieces. One day, perchance, I can work up the courage to make it.

*Day nine:*
Today I was in Thomas' wagon looking for some supplies that John and Blue required. I came upon a box that had a lovely log cabin quilt in it. I took it out to admire it and look at the wonderful construction of it. The blocks were unique; four log cabin blocks sewn together with fire red triangles going around the outside edges. I spread it out and a letter fell open at my feet. I saw it was from his Mother. I felt as if I was intruding and quickly folded it back into the quilt. Although it is hard for your eyes to not see the words on the page. She wishes that he were wed and she has several women chosen for him back home. I wish my eyes had not betrayed me so. I will concentrate on not knowing this.

# Chapter 16
## Whiskey, the Briber

THE LAST NINE DAYS THOMAS HAD spent searching for Elizabeth Bromont and the others. Thomas was perplexed as to how they could have disappeared. He had talked to many after the storm and no one had heard of this group of women and eight wagons. At least he didn't think they were in trouble or harms way, such news would have certainly traveled fast. He did not want Lucas to get wind of this or any outlaws, so he was cautious in his investigations. He mostly listened for conversation that would lead him to his cluster of females.

He sat in a tipped back chair outside the saloon as two men in military uniform started up the steps.

"And you're certain that the wagon train was all single women?" The blonde man with the fuzzy eyebrows asked.

"Yes," the tall one said, stooping his head to enter the door of the saloon. "I was there. They stopped in Fort Polk with Captain Sewell's and his wife. Then they just went on."

Thomas almost knocked his chair off of the two legs that it was on as he stood up. He couldn't believe it. Finally, word of the women. He quickly glanced around for Chet and entered the building himself. He walked straight over to the men in blue and ordered three drinks.

"Gentlemen, did I hear right that you saw a wagon train of women?"

The two soldiers cautiously looked at Thomas, with Chet now standing next to them. The blonde man remembered the captain's warning, and how not to speak openly about it.

Thomas saw the hesitation and realized the situation. "Let me introduce my friend, Chet; and I am Thomas Bratcher. We are employed by Lucas Mailly to lead his wagon train and freight to Fort Worth. In the storm last week," Thomas paused, feeling the embarrassment of losing his group. "We lost track of our charge."

The two men in blue looked at each other, not certain whether they ought to talk

"I would be grateful for anything that you can tell me." Thomas said to the young men.

"Yes," the tall one began. "Mr. Bratcher, I saw them at Fort Polk. They were with the captain. Their wagon arrived two days ago."

Thomas leaned forward anxiously waiting for him to continue.

"What else?" Chet asked.

"As I remember, it seems they had come across some trouble. They lost a wagon in one of the rainstorms, but they appeared to be faring themselves just fine."

"Was anyone hurt?" Thomas asked.

"The lady that was leading them, she was; but only a scrape on the head."

"Yes," the other man said. "The others seemed just fine. What I can't understand is how those fine ladies have managed on the trail.

But they're headed right for Indian country as it is now." He reached for his whiskey. "What's wrong with that pa of theirs?"

"How bad was she hurt?" Thomas asked

"She was banged up all right. Captain Sewell sent her to the Doc."

"Tell me where she was hurt."

"Her eye was purple and she had a big scrape down her check. As well her lip, it was cut."

Thomas poured himself another whiskey. "And what direction were they headed?"

"The Captain gave them a map and had some men of ours ride them to the edge of Texas."

"Just tell me where they left them and where they told them to go." Thomas asked again.

"Our men left Fort Polk and were going west to the Sabine Forest. I suppose that's where they camped, but that's all I know."

"Well then men, thank you for your help." Thomas stood to shake their hand.

"Good luck." The blonde man said. "And thanks for the drink."

Thomas and Chet both gulped down their whiskey and went for the door.

Once outside, Chet turned to Thomas. "I think we should cut across to the north of the Sabine. I know a place we can cross the river and find a spot to meet them, close to where the Rangers should be. I know of a stage station close to the Crockett Forest and Nacogdoches," Chet said. "Maybe, if we push it we can do it in a five day ride."

"How long do you think it will take them?" Thomas asked

"I'd say at least six," Chet replied.

Lucas Mailly had had a productive week. He was on his way to sign the final paperwork to complete the sale of his timber mill. He would be headed to his new home before long. The granddaughters would be surprised to see him so soon. He passed through town and stopped at the mercantile to see if his favorite tobacco had arrived. At the counter was a newspaper from up North. He picked it up and called out to Carl behind the register.

"Put this on my bill. Has my order arrived yet?" He never took his eyes from the paper where a big story was written about President Buchanan and the split of a nation.

He rolled the paper up and walked to Carl.

"Any news around here worth telling? I haven't been to town since the girls left."

"Well Lucas, everyone seems right afraid to hear of you letting all of them go alone like that. No kinfolk with them. And now, several young girls from around town have got the inkling to send off by themselves. You really opened a can of worms now, Lucas." Carl said seriously, over his half-rimmed glasses. "We never thought you would do it."

"Well, I did." He paused, as if grasping something. "And now! You better believe me. Have you seen this?" He said, pointing to the paper. "A war between the states. Our state will be in the middle of it too, mark my words. Have you read this article?" Lucas shook the rolled newspaper at him and walked quickly out the door.

He suddenly realized that he was walking fast. He was anxious to finalize the deal, especially before everyone got wise and abandoned the south.

Lucas had never cared much about what others thought of him. As long as the man from the good book was content with him, he was content too.

"Lucas, your tobacco." But Carl was too late. Lucas was already gone.

# Chapter 17
## Megan's Sewing Box

LIZ SHOOK THE REINS OF HER team and looked from under her bonnet, searching for a place to make camp. She watched Bear as he played and ran close with the wagons. Bear had learned quickly the routine of each day and no one had to worry for his whereabouts. He would run and take off into the thicket or trees and then come back; and when he didn't return, Luke would whistle for him and he would come quickly running.

Once camp was made, and everyone settled, Bear came out from the thick trees with an angry raccoon chasing him. Liz was afraid the animal might have rabies and would bite Bear.

"Blue, do you see him? Hurry! Over there." Liz called.

Bear was barking and tormenting the masked creature as he hissed on back legs at the dog.

"Luke, stay back." His mother commanded from the wagon seat "John, scare him off!"

John came around the wagon with his gun firing two shots in the air. The raccoon hurried off with Bear still at his heels. Luke whistled and the dog finally turned for home.

"That was funny seeing that raccoon chasing Bear like that." John said.

"I guess so," Liz returned. "I was afraid it would be a crazy one and cause us harm."

John heard her say as he walked away.

"And that is all we need, another sack of trouble."

It had turned out to be a sun-filled day, with only a few clouds that flit around overhead. The heavy branches on the trees were green and insisted upon shading them. The grass was picturesque with deep, thick blades. The rain of the past few days had turned the area into such rich colors. Liz felt a deep sense of happiness as the sun warmed her face and penetrated her brain like a drug.

Megan jumped from her wagon seat and twirled in a circle around the prairie of lush grass. "It is beautiful here!" She exclaimed. "What a gorgeous day to be a part of."

Abby walked over to look into the trees. "I have never seen a place like this. Is this still the Sabine forest?"

Abby was correct in the account of this being a beautiful part of the world, still untouched by civilization. The meadow at the edge of the forest was from a fairytale land. Her Mississippi home was pretty, but not like Riverton where her cousins lived and positively not anything like this place called the Sabine. They had traveled along the bottom of it after the soldiers left them and they now turned north to the Angelina River and Crocket forest.

Liz was busy soaking it all in. "Well, do you think our new home will continue this beauty? I believe that I like this new place more and more. I'm so glad we stopped early so we can enjoy this. We get there when we get there! No?"

Liz had loosed her chickens and they scratched and bobbed around the camp. The women were anxious to get the quilt pieces out and start their stitching. Emma pulled out her nine-patch squares that she had recently completed and inspected them carefully, pulling one block to the side that required to be ripped out and restitched. The triangle units that were to be sewn together and were placed in another stack that was quite smaller. She silently went to work on the repair. The colors she had chosen were browns and blues.

Abby had a few dark colors in her basket and decided to work on her appliqué. It was her favorite. She cut out the small flowers and leaves and then turned down the edges as she stitched it to the background piece. As soon as she saw the quilt that Megan had made from their Granny Claire, she knew that she had to make it too. Megan's reproduction was blue and she would choose darker scraps to complete her own. She trimmed the leaves from the scrap of green for the block.

Each woman sat silently in her own world of fabric, needle, and thread, engrossed in the wonder of creativity.

A myriad of red and brown triangle units came from Megan's quilt box. They were all precut and stacked neatly together inside a pecan wood box lined with velvet. The velvet held the pieces where they were intended to be once the quilt was finished. A gentleman caller had given the wooden box to Megan as a gift. She then lined it with the fabric and turned it into a project box. Megan never was too keen on any of the callers, the box, however, was a keeper. It was a rich, pecan color with carved trim and about twelve inches square and not too deep. The hinges were pewter. Megan had made a small needle cushion inside. Emma was intrigued by it.

"Megan," Emma said. "I will help you with all of those triangles you have in that Feathered Star. It will be a masterpiece once you've finished it."

Megan passed the box of triangles to her sister; as it went by Emma, she reached out to hold it.

"Tell me about this box?" She asked as her fingers passed over the carvings.

Liz jumped in and said. "It's from one of Megan's many callers. She received it as a gift. It came from Mr. Matthew Coldwell. He was a buyer that came to the mill often. He was a master craftsman of furniture back in North Carolina. He was quite handsome and wealthy. He was very intrigued with our Megan and carved the box himself."

Megan gave her sister a disapproving look and returned to her needle and thread.

"Well, what happened?" Emma asked, wanting to know more.

"He is gone and the box is here, that's all there is to it." Megan worked to move the topic along.

"Sometimes it is best for a relationship to come to an end...even when...they care about each other and all appears to be well."

Emma looked to her sister not understanding completely, but knowing not to continue the conversation further, she didn't say anything.

Liz took the box and picked out the pieces she would sew together for Megan. She smiled at her sister and asked:

"Will each star be the same?"

"Well, yes and no; the center of the stars are all different eight-inch stars and the larger feathered star will be blue, red or green, and with black tips. I think I will make it large with twelve feathered stars."

Megan started to become herself again as she spoke of her design. She accepted the box as Liz passed it back to her. As her fingers passed over the engraving on the inside of the lid, she could hear Matthew's deep voice as he gave it to her. His voice could melt you all the way to your toes. It was rich and comforting. She loved to hear it when he sang the hymns in church when he was in Lecompte doing business with her Grandfather. She could recognize it anywhere and it drew her

124

in like nothing she had ever known. She thought she would marry Matthew if he ever asked, and, in fact, he did ask her.

Then, her future mother-in-law came for a visit and almost immediately she knew she would never be the first lady in his life. She was going to talk with him that dreadful night when the moon was out so gorgeous and they fell asleep under the moonlight in the wagon. When they came up on the porch it was late, and there his mother sat. Mrs. Coldwell was ready to tear into Megan and tell her how she was a tramp and not good enough for her blue-blood son; Megan held her tongue.

Megan knew this would never change and that Matthew's mother would always be first. She would not have married him even if he had stayed. In the process, her heart and trust were broken and now she never stayed around a caller for long. When it began to get serious, she was gone, leaving the young men wondering where they went wrong.

The sun began to fade for the day and the sewing was not right as the light dissipated. Megan placed her needle in the special box and read the engraving that she normally passed right over. It read:

*To my special Megan, all my love, always, Matthew*

Megan stood and withdrew to her wagon.

# Chapter 18
## Cowboys

THREE COWBOYS SAT AROUND THE campfire, just a short distance from the Angelina River. The fire they had built was of a large size. They had gathered several thick logs and other kindling which they had arranged at the base of the fire pit. They then found tall branches which had dried and placed them so that they formed a teepee, connecting at the top and creating an intense furnace inside by which no wind or cold could pierce.

The remains of a trail supper were evident. The coffeepot jumped over the fire. Each man was dressed in the traditional trail attire; a cowboy hat made of straw for shade and air circulation was deemed the most necessary; the only time it was not worn was in desperation as it was swatted across the owner's leg in anger or frustration. Even when a lady was present the hat was only tipped slightly, just enough

127

to be recognized as politeness. In such occurrences, the cowboy's hand would go up toward the brim and be tipped in acknowledgement, usually in accord with a "ma'am," and a polite gesture. When a cowboy's hat was removed it was the utmost sign of respect, and such a privilege was not frequently handed out.

The cowboys that now sat around the fire-poking it and mesmerized by its flame-were wearing bandannas around their necks with long sleeved shirts tucked into denim jeans. They wore tatty cowboy boots made from animal leather and leather belts with heavy, serious buckles. All three had on a leather vest with the metal star of a Texas Ranger protruding with magnanimity out from the chest area, where his heart was.

The oldest cowboy, Tex-not as old as Lucas Mailly-was old enough to be the father of the women he was searching for. He wasn't a large man in stature, but in attitude and accomplishments you couldn't find much bigger. He was a legend with the Texas Rangers and respected across the territory. He wasn't sure why Lucas Mailly would send his family alone across the land, but he wasn't sure why a man would leave his family at all; it seemed odd to him. In reality, these sorts of questions were of little concern to him or his group, for they had a job to do.

As he sat thinking, near the fire, he didn't know where the ladies were, but his duty didn't allow him to agonize over such things; he intended to locate their wagon train and then bring them safely to the fort, accordingly.

He had never met Lucas before, but he liked him. Lucas spoke of his granddaughters as a man would his sons. Tex considered it gutsy, no less, to send the women with such sizable amounts of gold; he certainly wouldn't have done it.

Tex looked over to the two Rangers he had been riding with all day. He had rode with both before and was familiar with their work; he liked the way they handled themselves; they were professionals and had integrity, as most all Rangers had. Tex looked over to Jackson, who was in his mid thirties he would guess. He was tall and broad with a long handlebar mustache. Jackson won most of his battles by sheer intimidation. He rode a large black stallion that carried a lofty attitude that listened only to his commands. Jackson, and his stallion, Zeus, created myth and legend wherever they went. Even if his enemies knew that he was really only a gentle giant, they would certainly not want to chance it, and they rarely did.

Tex teased Colt that he was so young he was still wet behind the ears. Colt was actually twenty-one, but never told anyone; he was eighteen when he started riding with the Rangers, but he had only ever ridden with Tex and Jackson.

The two eldest cowboys met Colt when they came upon a Comanche raid of a traveling group. Wagons were burning and bodies lay everywhere with the deadly arrows of the Plains Indian. The Comanche were fierce and superb warriors; they could release six arrows to one shot of the white man.

Colt had come out with a colt revolver; he had an aim many could never master; he was a natural shot. In fact, the Colt revolver was made for the Rangers and the three of them were no match for the Comanche. Ever since then, Tex took him in and started calling him Colt, after the gun that saved them all that day. Colt's reputation had grown bigger than life over the years and Tex was the only one that dared tease him about his age. Colt still had a bone to pick with the world; he would not be intimidated after that wagon raid. His soft brown locks were long down his back and he kept them tied back with a leather strip. At times, it seemed, he was surprisingly similar to the savages whom he stalked. Tex and Jackson never asked Colt his real name; Colt never gave it. They also never learned where he got the Colt revolver, or how he discovered that he could shoot so well.

Tex uncorked the bottle of whiskey he was married to and brought it to his lips, taking a big swig. The bottle rested on his leg as he considered another.

"What's eatin' you?" Jackson asked his mentor.

"Ah, nothin' I can't handle."

It was silent for a few moments. The fire cracked.

"When do you see us finding that wagon train?" Jackson asked, and took the bottle from his friend's knee. Jackson rarely drank; although, he would take a swig now and then. Just now, as he took it, he didn't want a swig, but he thought it was a respectful way to take it from his mentor. Tex had a demon or two that haunted him and Jackson didn't want it showing up tonight. He had also seen his Captain this way before. Though it rarely happened, if ever, they were on duty and there was always the opportunity for danger.

"As we go north, we'll find them."

Colt stirred the fire and added another log. "Why are we sent to this group anyway? It doesn't make sense to me. We don't guard wagons and help them across the frontier; we pull them out of trouble after they find it…and they always do."

Colt had little sympathy for wagon trains. Few, in his mind, had business going west. He had seen too much.

Jackson knew it was hard on Colt, seeing wagon after wagon in trouble. He knew that it reminded him and took him back to the time when he had lost his family.

"Women have got no business on the frontier." Colt continued.

Tex lay back on his saddle and tipped his hat forward. "Jackson, take first watch. Colt you're next."

He turned his back to the fire and adjusted the bedroll under his shoulder. Jackson heard Tex mutter. "Damn, I miss my dog."

# Chapter 19
## Texas Rangers

T HE MAILLY PARTY HAD TRAVELED SEVERAL DAYS and still had not come across the Rangers; neither had they found Thomas nor Chet. Liz had the oddest feeling that all was well with them and that they would meet up at the Fort, if not sooner. She sometimes doubted this feeling, though.

Liz sat around the evening embers of the campfire. The open fire was soothing and an agreeable place for thinking; she missed her rocking chair and access to a sturdy oil lamp for sewing or reading her Bible. She thought about one of her favorite verses that she often recalled since Caleb had died. She recited it softly as she stirred the fire.

"On every side, we are pressed by trouble, we are crushed and broken. We don't comprehend. We are knocked down again…" She paused, took a deep breath and looked into the darkness of night and finished the verse. "But we get up again, II Corinthians 4:8."

Liz turned her head as she heard a noise and Megan appeared from the brush.

"Megan you scared me again. Someday you will get shot sneaking around like that."

Megan laughed and sat down by her sister.

"How many times do we get up?" She asked her.

"A righteous man may trip seven times, but each time they will rise again. Proverbs 24:17"

They looked at each other and smiled. Megan's hand went to Liz's face where she was bruised and banged up from the storm.

"You are looking better. How do you feel?"

"I try not to think what I must look like, but I do feel better."

"If you would ever sleep you would never know if I'm out in the dark or not."

Liz smiled.

"Do you miss home?"

"Do you?" Liz asked in return.

"Not really, but I do wonder if Grandpa is worried over us and if he got word somehow about our troubles?"

"He knew we would have trouble and maybe even get lost, but he thought we would have a little more help than we have had from Thomas and Chet. The only way we were to be alone like this was if someone was killed. He won't be gentle with them when he finds out. Though, I don't think it was their fault; it just happened."

"So you think they are alive out there looking for us?"

"Yes, I do; and most likely very upset with us for not making it easier."

They both laughed.

"Why do I need a man at all in my life? If I can get us across the prairie then I can make it on my own. I will have the mercantile and you can have your dress shop and we will be just fine. Luke is almost grown; I don't need to remarry for him. I feel like they are never there when you really need them the most. I have grown a hard heart and I know that. I don't want to be hurt again."

Megan stirred the fire a little and turned to face her sister. "You had a happy marriage with Caleb; don't dishonor him by thinking bitterly about marriage. You don't mean it. We just have not met suitable men. I'm simply saying to you, don't give up on Thomas; he loves you."

Megan hugged her sister. She stood and withdrew to her wagon for the night. Liz stayed and listened to the night creatures humming.

Liz was deep into the thoughts of self-pity and was not on guard to hear the approach of Colt as he entered her camp on foot. She stirred the fire and realized boots were in front of her and the fire. Startled, she looked up and gasped as she saw a man with his hat over his eyes and long hair. His leather holster sported two revolvers; he had a rifle in his hand with the butt of the gun up to his hip. Liz was nearly looking down the barrel.

"You're not too cautious." Colt stated.

"And you're rather brave, walking right into my camp like this." She stood quickly and thought of what to do. Blue and John had already retired for the night. "What do you want and who are you?"

"I could have killed you or..." Colt began.

"You might get one of us but you would never walk the same again." Megan's voice came from the brush and trees behind the wagon, hidden in the darkness.

Colt was unaware of Megan in the trees and wondered how he had missed her. He had watched the little group all day before reporting to Tex that he had found the women that they were searching for. It had grown very dark, and he observed them again before making the decision to go into the camp. He did not intend to frighten them or get himself shot. Tex and Jackson would sure have some fun with this situation if they knew.

"Just come out of the trees, lady." Colt sounded impatient. "I don't

133

want anyone hurt."

"You would like that, drop your gun and step away."
Colt lowered his gun and backed away. He was now in an area out of the fire's light, and neither woman could now see him. Megan squinted her eyes, but couldn't make out a figure.

"Step into the light." She ordered. "Now!"

"I don't want to hurt you, ma'am. I could have killed you by now. I've watched you all day. I know who you are. I am a Texas Ranger come to escort you to Fort Worth." He motioned to his badge, hidden by his hair, on his vest pocket.

Liz and Megan let out a heavy sigh of relief. Just then, Bear came running up to Colt with his tail wagging as if he were an old friend.

"Bear, you trader!" Liz stated as she watched the two. "How does he know you?"

"Yes," Colt laughed. "We became friends over by the ridge of rocks today. I was watching all of you and he came to me just like this."

Bear and Colt were playing as he got on one knee to pat the black dog. Megan appeared from the dark with her hand still on her gun, not completely wanting to let down her guard. Megan came and stood by her sister looking over what she thought was a man. He had as much unruly hair as the dog. They both looked at each other thinking the same thing. They had never seen a man with hair that long, tied and wrapped with a leather strap on each side of his head. It was too wavy for him to be Indian and his skin too light even though he was heavily tanned. His eyes were brownish green and not black as a redskin. Bear jumped on his shoulder and knocked him off balance as he squatted on the toes of his boots.

"Are you alone then?" Liz asked. "We were told that Tex would be our escort."

"Tex will be here. Jackson is riding with us too. They were...delayed... be along late morning. You two go on to bed, Bear and I will keep guard together."

Colt and Bear continued to play around as Liz and Megan slowly drifted to their wagon for bed.

Lucas Mailly was just gulping the last of his coffee as he made out his bedroll. It felt good to be on the trail again with his horse. He added another log, checked his mare and said his prayer. He was plenty tired; it had been a long time since he had covered twenty-five miles on horseback. He closed his eyes a happy man.

# Chapter 20
## The Angelina River

THOMAS WAS JUST FINISHING HIS CUP OF MORNING COFFEE and deep in thought. He couldn't understand how he could have missed Liz and the others. He was beside himself in frustration and embarrassment. He knew life was too short to waste any time. The code of the west was to do it while you still could. He would ask Liz to marry him as soon as he found her and he was determined to not lose her again. If they were married, he could take better care of her, he was sure of that.

"To-day is the day!" Chet announced as he approached Thomas and the coffee that was still fresh.

"For what?" Thomas asked.

"I feel it in my bones. We will meet up with the wagons today. I have done all the calculations and here along the river, we will find them." Chet motioned south.

Thomas looked the way he motioned.

"I don't know, but I hope you're right."

Thomas wished he had asked her before they left. He would not have lost them then, he would not have felt pushed to go after Chet when he went missing. Hindsight, of course, is always near perfect. He remembered back to the porch with Liz the day the wagons arrived. He thought Liz was going to tell him something that would let him know that she was willing to move on with her life. Thomas knew he loved Liz. He had hoped the trip would be the time where she could see that she loved him too. Things had not worked in his favor.

Chet moved the dirt over the fire with his boot and looked to Thomas who was pulling the belly strap of his saddle under his mare. Chet wondered what had all of Thomas' attention. They both leaped onto the back of their mounts and turned to find the others in the early morning light.

Early in the morning, Liz gathered the women together. They gathered up all the laundry and bathing supplies and informed the men that they would be back after while.

Colt had gotten acquainted with John, Blue and Luke over breakfast and enjoyed the two eggs from Liz's chickens. He never had two thoughts about the women going to the river. It was not his job to herd them or advise them of danger.

"Luke, does Bear know any commands?" Colt asked as he played with the black dog and a stick from the fire.

"He will come when I whistle and he growls to warn us of danger." Luke answered and walked closer to the two.

"That one doesn't count." Colt teased. "He let me come right into your camp last night."

Luke smiled and kicked at the log where Colt sat.

"Do you know how to teach him some?" Luke asked.

"I sure do. Tex, my Captain, had a great dog. He knew all sorts of things that Tex had taught him. I think Bear could learn them. Heck, I already taught him to roll over yesterday when he was hanging out with me at the ridge.

"You want to teach verbal commands and hand ones, too. Some time you may want him to do something and you don't want any one to hear you give the command. We can teach this dog to save your life. Tex had the best dog I ever saw; he would get his horse or run one off. He knew to stay, hide, fetch, and attack or take away the weapon from some outlaw's hand. She even would sneak into camp and pull out the holsters of sleeping bandits. She was a great dog, even had a Ranger badge."

"Where is that dog now?" Luke wondered.

"She was killed." Colt said with remorse. "Her name was Allie. Don't ask Tex about her, it puts him in a grumpy mood."

"I don't know why they are always looking for a good spot to take a bath; at least they don't make me go." Luke protested as he looked toward the trail they took to the river.

"Where is your pa? Why did he not come with you?" Colt quizzed Luke.

"My Pa died at the mill."

"What happened to the other men that came along?"

"Oh, they're not dead; we lost them."

"How could you lose them?"

"We were separated by the storm."

"That's unfortunate."

"Yes," Luke agreed. "I'm going to gather more firewood."

The water was cool but comfortable once one got use to it. Each woman took off her dress and scrubbed it on the rocks and then laid it over a bush to dry. The garments would dry quickly in the hot Texas sun and be ready to put back on.

"Are you sure no one is around?" Megan asked glancing about them.

"Yes." Liz answered as she waded to her knees.

Megan and Emma looked about and started to untie their camisoles.

"Are you sure?" Emma asked looking at Liz.

"Emma don't." Abby said as she wading into the water with hers on.

"Abby that is just your prim and proper school teacher attitude. Go ahead; let your hair down too." Megan implored

Liz looked at Abby. "It's fine if you want to. I'm going to wash it and then put it back on as I swim and wash my hair."

The ladies swam and enjoyed the cool water over their sore muscles. They were good swimmers and loved the water. Grandpa Lucas had taught them how to swim back when they were all very young. The lavender soap bubbles were applied to milky white skin; they washed their hair and it squeaked as it went between their fingers.

"This feels so good I don't want to get out." Megan sighed as she floated about. "I think my clothes are dry now." Megan reached up to the rock to check and see.

"Oh, you were the smart ones." Liz realized. "I should have put my camisole on the rocks to dry also and not swam about in it. I will have to wait a little longer to let mine dry. You go ahead I will just swim across and back. They should be dry." She skimmed out of it and placed it on the edge of the rock that protruded over the water.

The three women dried off with the heavy cloth and dressed quickly in the fresh cotton clothing. Their hair was then combed and wrapped in the towel to dry. They felt refreshed and went around the bend to camp as Liz reached the other side of the deep river.

Tex and Jackson had arrived at the wagon camp shortly after the women had retreated to the river. John and Blue quickly made friends with the Rangers. Luke was impressed with the fact that three Texas Rangers would be riding with them all the way into the fort. The three of them standing together with all of the western attire and metal badges was rather impressive to the group. Luke noticed that the badge that Tex wore had a small dent in it. He imagined that a bullet in a fierce battle had made the mark.

"The women folk are back." John announced.

"Where is Mrs. Bromont?" Colt asked as he counted only the three.

"She will be back in a moment. Her clothing is still a little wet. She decided to swim across and back one more time to give them a bit more time in the sun." Megan said to the group. She noticed the two other men that must be Tex and Jackson, the Rangers.

"Hello, I'm Megan Ronnay. These are my cousins. Miss Abby and Emma Wilkes of Mississippi. We are the granddaughters of Mr. Lucas Mailly." Megan held out her hand and motioned to the two grown women with damp hair.

Tex and Jackson reached to the brim of their cowboy hats and made a respectful nod toward the women.

The sky was a clear blue with large billows strewn about with hallow centers. The sunrays broke through the cracks in the clouds and strong, direct rays shot down in a serious attempt to be glorious. The streams of light grabbed Luke's attention and he couldn't believe what he saw as he looked toward the spectacular view. Just then, Jackson turned to see what Luke was so stunned about and saw two young Indian braves on horseback looking down upon the river.

"Miss Megan, show me your sister." Jackson took Megan's arm and pulled her toward him and the river.

His legs where so much longer than hers that she felt like she was flying across the earth to the river where she had last seen her sister. Megan never heard or saw him take his gun from the holster as they sprinted down the bank.

Liz was standing in the shallow water, her camisole still damp and clinging to her. Water was dripping from her face and hair as it hung down her back. The sunrays came down in spears from the random clouds and bounced around the water in glistening streaks. She was gorgeous, almost heavenly looking with streaks of blonde in her hair. A third young brave stood beside his painted pony, barely in the water, mesmerized by her radiance. Liz stood calm, but was stunned when she opened her eyes and saw the Indian so close to her. No sound escaped from her, she was frozen. He reached out to touch her to make sure what he saw was real. She gasped as his hand made contact with her face and neck.

The young Indian heard Jackson making his way down the rocky path like a large bear stumbling down hill. He turned briefly to see that Jackson did have the size of a grizzly and perhaps the temperament too. He turned back to Liz and then ran towards his pony. On the opposite side, the other two were already making their way across the water to the safety of the thick trees.

Megan was down to the water first and reached for the drying cloth as she approached Liz in the water. Liz was mildly traumatized by the experience; it was her first time to see an Indian. Megan wrapped the cloth around her and pulled her from the water.

"Liz, are you hurt? Look at me. Are you fine?" Megan held her sister by the shoulders trying to get her to talk normal to her.

"I...never saw him approach. I opened my eyes and he was so close. He touched me."

"Did he hurt you?"

"I'm not hurt. I'm frightened. I just need a moment."

Jackson was now near and held out the dress that was nearly dry.

"Miss Megan," He stated, turning his back on the two women. He glanced over to the wooded area where the braves disappeared. "You scared them off, Mrs. Bromont. I think they thought you were some water goddess or something," He chuckled. "Wait till Tex hears about this. It's a good thing someone didn't get stupid and try to shoot one of them young boys. They might be so shaken that they don't even tell no one."

Liz quickly regained her composure and pulled the wet hair from the back of her dress. She looked to Megan with a questioning expression, as to say, "Who is that huge man." Megan quickly spoke up.

"Jackson, you may turn around and meet my sister, Elizabeth Bromont."

Jackson faced her with one foot on a large rock and his colt revolver still in hand. He glanced down to the gun and placed it back in its holster on his leg.

"Mrs. Bromont, good to meet you alive. Let's get back to camp and you can get acquainted with the others."

Tex was relieved as he saw the three climbing up the hill, and that he had heard no shots from the river. It was strange to have a midday attack, but it could happen-especially with young, eager braves trying to prove themselves.

Megan took hold of the introductions, "Tex, I would like for you to meet my sister, Mrs. Caleb Bromont."

Liz stepped toward the aging cowboy. She liked what she saw in his eyes; he had wrinkles at the corners of his eyes when he smiled at her. He took her hand in a hearty handshake. His spurs jingled when he took a step. She could see wisdom and sadness in his features.

"Tex, it's good to finally catch up with you. I'm Elizabeth Bromont. Forgive our appearance as we were not expecting Rangers or Indians today." She smiled; she could feel her heart beating normal again.

"Well, looks like they are gone. This is Jackson here, and this is Colt. All good men, they are. Mrs. Bromont we will get you all safely to Fort Worth in a few days."

"Already, thank you so much. We are very grateful."

"I know that you've lost some of the others in your group."

"Yes."

"I've heard of no mishaps in the territory."

Liz and Megan both nodded.

"It happens more often then you might imagine that groups get split along the trail. They know where you are headed, so that is well, at least. We will keep an eye out for them."

"Thank you, Mister Tex." She stumbled with his name.

"Tex is fine, Mrs. Bromont."

Elizabeth nodded to him and smiled. She walked over to the campfire to dry and braid her hair. The other women followed.

The evening was now late and once again Liz was by the evening embers, unable to sleep. Tex strolled to the fire from his horse and sat on a log across from Liz.

"Colt's on guard duty; you don't have to stay up."

Liz sipped her tea.

"Can't sleep?" He asked.

"It seems to be a problem that I have acquired."

Tex took out a thin paper and held it gently in his left hand. He reached behind his vest, to his shirt pocket, and pulled out a pouch of tobacco; he tapped a little of it onto the paper. It then went back in the pocket with one hand, the other still carefully holding the paper with the tobacco. He brought it up to his mouth and licked the paper down one side. It was then rolled into a cylinder and clung together. He ran it under his nose and took a deep breath, breathing in the pungent aroma. They were both silent.

"What is it like being a lawman? Do you not want to stay put some where?"

Tex picked up a small twig and placed it at the edge of the fire to ignite it. He used the burning twig to light the end of his cigarette. He pulled a big breathe from the tobacco and exhaled a smoke ring that floated up.

"Not much difference in a lawman or an outlaw Miss. They both stay on the move. I just think a lawman dies with honor and the outlaw just dies."

"Do you ever wish that you could have a place of your own or a family too? I'm so anxious to get settled again. This on the road…it's enough for me."

Tex sat quietly and smoked his cigarette that was now smaller. He looked at the end of it and moved his tanned fingers closer to the unlit end. His hand now rested on his knee where he flicked the ashes and he looked at Mrs. Bromont.

"I had a family once, a good woman and four girls. They had golden curls, something like yours. We had little ranch too." He was silent for a while. Liz sat wondering about this man and his sorrow.

"I'm sorry for your loss." Liz stated in a comforting voice.

"Oh, don't feel sorry for me. It is my fault that I don't have them and the ranch. I'm an old cowboy; I have paid for my choices."

Liz was confused. "What do you mean? I thought they were dead."

"One day, I just got on my horse and road off. I didn't mean to leave…I just never went back, and I never sent word. The pull of the west got me. Once I realized that I wanted to go back, it was too late; the girls were almost grown and life moved on. Allie remarried. They thought I was dead; I decided to leave them with that memory." He paused and flicked the butt of his cigarette into the fire after he took the last puff.

Liz watched and listened to his story. The cigarette glowed as he dragged on it. It sparked pretty red ambers as it bounced from a rock at the fire's edge. She saw a tanned wrinkled face with a two-day stubble. He rubbed his shoulder and made a small moan. He then stretched out his legs, his boots daringly close to the flame.

"Are you hurt…I have some ointment." Liz offered the aging cowboy.

"Thank you, I am fine. Just an old wound from breaking a stubborn mustang a few years back."

Liz looked back to the fire.

"Rain comin' in it seems; my shoulder knows."

Tex looked at Mrs. Bromont "Sorry about the loss of your mister. You know for sure he is dead?"

Liz thought it was a strange question to ask; she looked over to him. "Many of the workers witnessed the accident," she answered quietly.

Liz felt very tired at the moment and excused herself to go to bed. As she stood to make her way to the wagon she saw lightening in the distance.

"Goodnight Tex."

Tex stood and looked to the rumble of clouds in the dark night sky. He went to his supplies and placed them in the wagon Thomas had used. He pulled his rain slicker from his saddlebag. His rifle was lying on the wagon seat and he picked it up as he turned to relieve the ranger on midnight guard duty.

As he entered the blackness that surrounded the camp, Tex pulled the cork from a small bottle in his hand. He felt the first rain drop on his cheek. He sat down on a rock.

# Chapter 21
## *Found*

THE MOON WAS TURNING FULL AGAIN and the clouds in the distance were full of striking power. Thomas and Chet stopped only for a few moments to stretch their legs and give their ponies a break. They had decided to continue on since the night had a light and the clouds did not block it. Thomas had considered that it might be possible for them to see the light from a campfire; perhaps, they could be more easily directed to the Mailly wagons. Chet was certain that they had to be near; Thomas wanted to believe that as well.

They were at the top of a small hill. With the help of the reflective moon, they could almost peer into the night's vastness. Thomas reached into his saddlebag and pulled out his rain slicker. A gust blew in and Chet looked around to see if the storm clouds had come upon them yet. He pushed his cowboy hat down on his head and reached for his coat, looking up at the sky.

"It's just a few clouds, let's keep riding." Thomas said to Chet as he surveyed the sky again.

Chet agreed and quickly mounted his pony.

They rode toward the illuminated clouds, looking for any sign of a camp. The sky rumbled like a low drum. When the clouds lit up again, they could both see a small trail of smoke circling up to the night sky. Thomas looked over to see if his friend saw it. They leaned forward and spurred their mares into a full gallop. The raindrops began to hit the slickers harder.

Jackson had come to relieve Tex from guard duty and saw the evidence of riders approaching quickly.

"Do you see it?" Jackson asked as he stood next to his friend and boss.

He shook his head and said. "I have watched them for a short time. They are headed to us… guess they saw our fire. I'm assuming they are looking for us; they seem anxious to approach even with a storm."

"They are not hiding their approach; I don't think they are dangerous." Jackson added.

"Are the women asleep?"

"Yes."

"Only in case, I will go and wake the men. Do you have many rounds with you?"

"I've thirty rounds."

"I'm anxious to meet these two. How do you loose eight wagons for almost a month." Tex was not impressed.

Tex went back to camp to alert the men of approaching riders. Tex turned around and called out to Jackson:

"Once they've been here awhile, approach from the east."

Jackson nodded.

Thomas slowed his animal as they got closer to camp. He was excited to find them; he was sure it was them. Though, he had not taken into consideration the hour, and did not want to frighten them by barreling into camp. Chet took the cue and slowed his pony as well.

"Be on the look out for a guard; we don't want to scare John or Blue as we approach."

"Good thinkin'." Chet replied.

They could see into camp now and saw John, Blue and three others, all with their guns up in the air. They stepped down from the horses and called out as they approached the outer ring of camp.

"John! Blue!" Thomas called out from the morning darkness. "We are a-coming in."

"It is them!" John announced.

Tex and the others lowered their weapons and stepped out into the open as the two entered with damp rain slickers and hearty smiles. They exchanged introductions, handshakes and firm slaps on the back as the group welcomed each other.

"Thomas!" Luke hollered as he climbed from the wagon and ran to greet him.

Luke and his dog reached them at the same time; they nearly knocked Thomas over as they greeted him.

"It's good to see you Thomas! What happened? Where have you been? We had a tornado, and mom had a black eye"

John and Blue laughed over Luke's excitement and summary of the trip. Thomas ruffled Luke's bed hair and laid his hand over his shoulder. "It sure is good to see you, Lucas."

Liz was awakened by all of the commotion, and now walked closer to the group to see exactly what was the matter.

"Thomas! Oh, gracious! Thomas, is that you?"

"It's me Liz. I found you!"

Liz came running and immediately gave Thomas a big huge. She threw her arms around his neck and held him tight. Thomas put his arms around her waist and pulled her closer to him. Liz started to cry.

"I was beginning to worry, Thomas. We didn't know where you were."

149

Liz turned to Chet and hugged him, too.

"I can't believe you made it back to us. Are you both all right?"

"Yes," Thomas answered. "We're both fine; we're very tired."

"You really are here, Thomas! I almost can't believe it!"

"Is the coffee on?" Thomas asked.

The group moved to the coffeepot at the fire and began to pour the coffee. As the sun came up, they exchanged each story and began to piece the puzzle together on how they had lost each other for so long.

"Then the storm came and erased all the tracks and chance of us following you." Chet added at last.

"They went too far south while the others went west," Jackson added.

"Miss Emma, I sure wish you could have sewn me up." Chet pulled his thick long hair away from his forehead, revealing his healing but wide gash atop his forehead.

Emma stood and went close to inspect the cut. She placed her hand on his chin to tilt his head in the early light for a better look.

"Yes," Emma said, confidently. "I believe I could have helped more with the scaring. At least it is close to your hairline, it can't be seen really."

"What luck!" Chet said.

Emma let his hair fall back over the cut; she looked at her patient thoughtfully.

"Chet, are you certain that you are well? I'm not so sure." She placed the back of her hand to his forehead again to feel for a fever. "I think you feel warm." She now leaned closer to place her cheek on his forehead.

As the morning sun came up, the group sat talking about all they had encountered since they had last seen each other. In some ways, they felt like a family and enjoyed the interaction.

Thomas was happy man as he sat next to Elizabeth, and she was at ease with him. It felt good to be together. Luke sat on the other side of Thomas. To someone who didn't know any better, they looked like a family, sitting so close to each other and talking. Thomas sat with his arm along the back of Liz, resting on the wagon wheel.

# Chapter 22
## The Peddler

THE PEDDLER'S WAGONS WAITED at the gates of Fort Polk. The burly, old peddler was anxious to be let in. Captain Sewell's wife always usually offered him a good meal and a place to stay for the night. He knew that the baby would have arrived since he was last at the Fort, and he had brought a gift for the new little one. He had to trade for the buggy as soon as he saw it at the widow's farm; he had given a good price for it. The widow, for some reason, was not willing to give the buggy up to the Irish peddler.

Captain Sewell arrived at the gate as it was swung open by the two privates.

"Hello, Mr. Skelly; my wife is anxious to see you." He said proudly.

"Oh, and congratulations! Your baby must have been born by now." He spoke in his Irish brogue. "The wee one's name?"

The Captain was on horseback, riding next to the wagon; as the wheels rotated, a musical sound bellowed from the clanking of the peddler's inventory.

"Samantha, after her grandmother."

"Oh, Saamaanthaa! A fine name!"

Mrs. Sewell was waiting on the wooden porch. The wagon finally stopped in front of her. Once the clanging of the wagon stopped, she said:

"Mr. Skelly, so wonderful to see you again!"

"Yes," he said. "And yourself as well. I brought a gift for your new wee daughter."

The peddler had stepped down from the wagon and stood presenting the royal carriage.

"Oh my! Mr. Skelly, this is simply too much! It is wonderful!" She exclaimed as she pushed it on the porch and circled around.

"No no no, I insist." He answered, proudly.

She threw her arms around his neck and hugged the old man firmly. She placed a hearty kiss on his plump cheek. He promptly blushed.

"You're a lucky man, Mr. Skelly. Such a wonderful buggy." The Captain smiled as he watched his wife enjoy the gift.

"No, you're the lucky one, my friend."

"I must leave you two now to your trading. I will see you at supper." The Captain kissed his wife and withdrew to his office.

"Mr. Skelly, come inside at once. I have a sweet treat and some tea for you, if you'd like."

"Sounds wonderful, Mrs. Sewell."

"I can't wait to see what you have for me."

They walked inside and sat down at a large, low table. After the peddler had eaten two slices of cake, Mrs. Sewell asked him:

"I would like something for my husband. Do you have something particularly special? It's our anniversary and I would like for him to have something nice."

He leaned back in his chair, thinking; his finger came up to his chin.

"I have just the thing." He sprang from his chair, went straight to door and climbed into the back of his wagon.

He returned to the door holding a velvet bag. He placed it in her hand and she sat down. She opened it carefully and a gold pocket watch slid into her open hand.

"My it is exquisite."

She admired it as the shiny chain twisted between her fingers. It was etched with a scroll on the cover. She held it to her ear and could hear it ticking and the joints motioning inside.

"Of course, I will take it."

"Wonderful."

"What will you take for it?"

The peddler looked up and tapped his chin. He spoke quickly in his thick, Irish brogue "Well, it's had my eye for sometime now as you know."

"This quilt? Will you take a quilt for trade?" She motioned to the bridal wreath quilt; it lay over the back of a chair, folded and neat.

For all Mrs. Sewell had done for the peddler, he considered such a trade repayment for a year of lodging and food. Additionally, from experience, he had learned that a new quilt, as this one was, was a great rarity to traders; and for a quilt as it was-precisely made, and meticulous, was her work-he was certain to make a trade for it once he traveled farther north, where it was colder.

The peddler looked upon the circles of the bridal wreath quilt representing the wedding ring and admired the tiny stitches in the hand quilting. Each circle had over seventy pieces in it and was a different color of blue, red, green, gold and brown.

"You've just completed it; have you not?"

"Yes."

"I can't get for it what I could the pocket watch; but you've done so much for me that I could never turn you down. It's a deal."

"Very good, you will stay for supper then, and be our guest for the night?"

"I will accept the offer for a meal and lodging. You are very gracious to me, Mrs. Sewell. May the blessings be on you and yours."

"Where will you be going when you leave here?"

"I think I will head north, to the fort in Texas called Worth."

# Chapter 23
## The Way West

**T**EX AND THOMAS BOTH AGREED that they could travel faster if the men drove the wagons. The women would be given a break. Fort Worth was not many days away. Their main concern was that they wanted to make it through the Commanche territory safely, with the women and the gold.

The horses were tethered to their appointed wagons. Colt would be in the first wagon and it would be full of gold. He would drive alone; he was content to do it this way. Colt was told to keep a sharp eye out for any sign of danger; he had his Colt revolver traveling by his side. He checked his ammunition. He was proud to have such a valuable responsibility, looking after the gold.

The next would be Thomas and Liz, the latter whom was contented only to watch the land as it rolled past and comment to Thomas how different it seemed from Lecompte. She wondered what vegetables would grow in her garden and worried over putting in a few late ones. Thomas assured her that he would help her find a suitable location. Late in the day, Liz relaxed; she had fallen asleep on Thomas' shoulder, as the wheels rolled on and crunched over rocks.

In the third wagon rode Megan and Chet, sitting side by side. Megan took the opportunity of rest to work on the feathered star blocks as she chatted with her friend.

Behind Megan and Chet, were Abby and Tex. Abby had befriended Tex the evening before, around the campfire, she had asked if she could ride with him. Tex agreed. She was intrigued by his stories. His life and stories were full of such adventure, often times mixed with despair. Many of his stories were sad, though some were uplifting. He had experienced a great deal working the prairie and woodlands; it was his home now. Abby considered such an opportunity to ride with him a treasure. She could gain knowledge from him, she thought, knowledge which she could pass on to her students as she gained a more thorough understanding of history, as it was being written. She wrote many of his stories in her journal.

Abby was most interested in Tex's stories about many of the Indians he had encountered. She was afraid of the Indians, as most people were. Abby felt that, even though the Indians were savages, perhaps, there was something to be learned from them. As they rode next to each other, Tex thought of his daughters which he had left behind so many years ago. He wondered if they were as talented or sweet as Abby.

In the fifth wagon were Jackson and young Emma. They chatted to make the time pass more quickly. Emma quilted as they rode. She counted her blocks; she was confident that, in the days that followed, she could complete all that were left, as though she were in some quilting competition which no one else knew about.

Luke and John were next in line with Blue picking up the rear. Blue was pleased to be in his own wagon again. With Thomas now back, he

felt relieved of his command of duty, or what little command he had
had over the women.

As they rode north and slightly west, the group made exceptional
time. The trail was worn and easier to travel. After several days of
riding, they came upon a cavalry brigade herding camels. The Mailly
women had never seen the desert animal; they were charmed by its
humps and unwieldy waddle. Tex had told them that the army often
times used camels if they planned to travel into west Texas; they were
more water-conscious than horses, though slower.

One evening, as the group camped, Miss Megan convinced two
soldiers to let her ride a camel; she rode through both camps, riding
between the humps of the lofty animal. Tex and Thomas went into the
army camp and informed the officer in charge to keep his troops in
their own camp. As the days followed, the two groups continued in the
same direction, although the Mailly train moved ahead more quickly.

From the hills, a small hunting band of Comanche watched the
strange group of animals as they went along. They were amazed by the
beast which they had never before seen. The next morning they
followed the buffalo herd that passed by, but caused no problems to
the wagon train or soldiers.

After supper one evening, Tex reported that they would be
approaching the fort in the morning. Liz stood up and threw her arms
around him and kissed his weathered cheek. In celebration, Chet
pulled out his bottle of homemade sourmash and passed it around the
fire. Tex held the bottle a little longer than the others and then
watched it as it made its way back to Chet. The women passed it along
without drinking, except for Megan who took a small taste.

The group decided to wake early in the morning.

The women of Fort Worth were gathering their sewing supplies into their baskets as Katie Longmont stood over the red schoolhouse quilt.

"It really is very nice." Katie said with approval.

The group of ladies had done a fine job on their blocks and now the quilting was complete too.

"Katie…do you mind sewing the binding by yourself? I can come by next week when Henry goes into town." Her friend Becky told her.

"It is fine. I have plenty of time to finish it before our new teacher arrives. It was such a grand idea to require each student to make a block with their name in it."

Katie continued to look the quilt over with anticipation for their children's education. The two women took Abby's schoolhouse quilt out of the quilting frame.

# Chapter 24
## The Fire

T HE SUN WAS UP AND IT WAS a new day; but not just another day on the trail, for today was the day that they would see their new home. For months, Liz had waited for this day; she was excited and nervous that it was finally upon them. The weather had chosen to be sunny.

Liz tied the bow of her bonnet as though it were a Sunday hat, and walked to the side of the wagon to see if the others were ready. About that time, Tex called out his usual two-minute warning to saddle up and leave.

Thomas spotted Liz as she came around to the wagon. Her hair was in a long braid down her back; the sun brought out her strands of gold which occasionally appeared in its light. Thomas admired her as she took a step towards him.

"Good morning, Thomas." Liz said with excitement evident in her voice.

"Good morning," he said. "Are you set to go?"

"Why yes, I am."

"Good, I will help you into the wagon."

Thomas helped her up and took his seat aside her on the wagon bench. She straightened out her skirt as if she were going to a ball in a fine carriage. She nibbled on the side of her lip and placed her hands in her lap with her leather gloves. She looked for Tex to give his command to move out. Bear raced by the wagon barking; he, too, could feel the excitement of the morning.

"Did Tex say it would be long before we see the edge of town?" Liz asked as the wagon took a jerk and started rolling.

"Not too long. He said late morning, I believe."

"I just want to soak it all in, the smell, sights and sounds. I never moved before; I was only six when we went to Lecompte to live with my grandfather." She paused and looked at her hands. "I was so young, Thomas; and so scared. We had just lost our parents in the fire; and suddenly, Megan was my responsibility."

"I can't imagine," Thomas said.

"My mother was pregnant then. I remember my father, telling me to take care of Meggy; he went back into the house to get them. I saw the fire everywhere and he disappeared into it. Just as he entered, the roof came down on them. Some people from town came when they saw the smoke and flames; they found us huddled together in one of granny's quilts. It was the only belonging we saved from the fire. It was too late to save the house or anyone in it." Liz looked away.

Thomas had never known what happened to Liz's parents. He listened in silence and imagined what it was like for the two small girls.

Thomas reached for her hand and held it.

"The pastor put us on a stage and paid our way to Lecompte. There was a note pinned to my green dress. The pastor's wife made us the dresses out of green fabric with vines and red flowers; they had red buttons on the bodice. Megan twisted one of her buttons off on the stage and cried. The pastor said that it was a good idea for us to look nice, that it would go in our favor to find a good home. They did not know if an old man would want to raise two little girls. Lucas was in town the day the stage arrived and saw us get off in the street. The note told him about the fire and the death of our parents. It seemed like days that we just sat on the porch in his lap. We all just cried and rocked...two little girls curled up in their grandfather's lap. I remember Megan saying, in her cute little baby voice, 'don't cry anymore pappy, we will take care of you.' She took the skirt off her green dress and wiped his tears away."

"Do you know what started the fire?" Thomas asked.

"Yes." Liz answered. "Momma's nightgown was in the fire. She was ready for the baby to come and she wasn't sleeping well. Somehow, her nightgown got in the fire and she was on fire. She was afraid and didn't know what to do. She ran in the house making it worse. I heard her screaming and falling over things. She told me to get Megan out of the house and get daddy from the barn. We had been sleeping and Megan wouldn't get up. As we struggled to get out, I saw her burning. The fire was everywhere."

Thomas placed his gloved hand on her knee. "Liz, I'm so sorry. I never knew."

"I don't know that I've ever told anyone before."

"Not even Caleb?" He asked surprised.

"No, we never spoke of it." Liz looked at Thomas, realizing how odd it sounded.

"I'm sorry. I didn't intend to have a depressing story. This is a happy day." Liz placed her hand over Thomas' and smiled; she looked over to the green hills and trees that stretched across the Texas prairie.

Together, they rode into Fort Worth.

**JODI BARROWS** is a nationally known quilting teacher, speaker and writer. She currently lives in the North Texas area. Over the past twenty years, Jodi has remarkably touched thousands of quilters throughout the world with her unique method called Square in a Square®. Her point of view provides the quilter with the freedom to create most any quilt design with speed and accuracy.

Jodi has spoken to quilting audiences throughout the United States, Canada, and Australia. She has appeared as a guest on several quilting shows, including TNN's Aleene's Creative Living, TNN's Your Home Studio, Perfecting Patchwork on Family Net TV, and PBS series with Kaye Wood. HGTV has shown her commercial on the quilting techniques she has developed on the Simply Quilts show.

The Square in a Square® system is a process that anyone can implement in most any design. Jodi has written sixteen books (ten of which have been on the best seller's list), two novels, produced four tools, two video/DVDs and five teacher's books. Additionally, she has a pattern book and fabric line based on a fiction novel she wrote from the 1856 time period entitled "Leaving Riverton."

She also has a Certified Teacher's Program in the United States and Canada. Jodi has had numerous quilts appear in McCall's, The Quilter, Quick and Easy Quilt World, House of White Birch Publications, Quilter's Newsletter Top Ten New Products, Leisure Arts Scrappy Bed Quilts 2003, Round Bobbin Quilting Professional, and a Featured Teacher in the Traditional Quilter.

Jodi has been commissioned to compose quilts for many state and national organizations as well as working with the Kansas Historical Society. She has been active in guilds as well as owning several crafting and sewing related businesses over the years. Jodi was raised in southwest Kansas, has 2 grown sons, and is married to Steve, her high school sweetheart.

**Square In A Square** • 1613 Lost Lake Drive • Keller, Texas 76248
TOLL FREE 1-888-624-6260 FAX 817-605-7420 EMAIL snsjodi@yahoo.com • WEB www.SquareInASquare.com

# A Sample Chapter from our Next Book

"I'm Anna Parker; welcome to Fort Worth. We are so excited to have you here!"

The four Mailly granddaughters gathered close to Anna and introduced themselves. She gave them a hug as she welcomed each one.

"Please don't be too overwhelmed by our excitement of your arrival. We are just anxious to get our little community up and going again. It has been quite concerning with the fort post moving on west. You and your commitments represent life to our town and we are thankful to you," Anna explained.

Liz and the other women knew they were welcomed in the area but had not realized fully that they were the new life for the town.

Anna began to lead them in the direction of their new buildings and explained a little more to them as they walked down the boarded sidewalks of Fort Worth, Texas. A small group of citizens followed and listened to every word.

"This is the place where we kept our supplies and these three buildings are yours for the mercantile and Megan's sewing business. They are all yours to do with as you wish. Also, the captain's quarters have the best living conditions. You can call them home."

Anna paused to let her words soak in. She searched each face looking for their thoughts.

Liz was scared but excited. Her mercantile was standing before her. She could see with her mind's eye and visualize shelves with an abundance of supplies. Yard goods, threads, lace and buttons lay in the center. On the back wall, sugar, coffee, beans and hard tack.

Small red check curtains hung at the windows and two double doors with a fresh coat of red paint swung open with warm greetings to every customer. Over the porch, the sign read "Mailly Mercantile". Rocking chairs set out front.

Liz came out of her thoughts as she heard Anna's voice again.

"We would like to have all of you for supper tonight. I will have some sandwiches sent over for you so you can get started right away on settling in. I am so glad to have you here safely. We've planned a Texas cookout for you and will get word out for Sunday. Parker will introduce you to the families of Fort Worth!"

Anna was as sweet as they had all hoped for. She had a soft, soothing voice and her dark hair was very curly. It was pulled up away from her face with a gold hair comb. It fell loosely down her back in a storm of curls.

Liz thought Anna was about Abby's age but not as tall.

"Anna, Abby is my cousin from Mississippi; she is the new teacher Pastor Parker has hired." Liz placed her hand on Anna's arm.

"Oh! In my excitement, I completely forgot about the school. I'm sure the school board members would like to show you the classroom area. My husband is out on a call. Do you mind waiting for Parker to arrive?" Anna asked.

Abby was glad to see all of the emotion about the school. They were definitely wanted in this little town.

"We have plenty to do. I can wait," Abby replied.

"I will send him over as soon as he returns. This is so exciting. I have waited forever to have more women here." Anna reached right over and gave Abby a hug. When she finally released the new school marm, the men were ready to start unloading the wagons, dusty from the Louisiana trail.

"This is Smithy," Anna stated. "He will have these fine gentlemen get you unloaded. Just direct them."

Anna waved goodbye and walked back down the street from where she came.

John turned to Blue with a smile and said, "Oh, Liz can direct you all right."

These two had worked at the Mailly timber mill for years. They now wanted the chance to move west with the family. John and Blue both respected Lucas and Thomas and would continue their employment.

"Well, we aren't in Louisiana any more." Liz thought as she looked about from the wooden steps in front of the new location for her mercantile.

There was a dirt road out front that disappeared in both directions. On each side of the mercantile, were wooden buildings left behind by the Calvary. A huge pecan tree with its branches reaching twenty feet or more in each direction was across from where she stood. Playing in the nice grassy area beneath the tree where two squirrels surveying the new group of citizens. The church and the new schoolroom were on down from the pecan tree. On the same side of the street where Liz stood and down to the right, was the smithy. Next to the smithy was a set of corrals, which held two mules and one stallion with a long black mane. He pawed at the edge of the gate and shook his head. His mane hung in the air and demanded attention.

At the end of her boardwalk and back to the left, the street turned and there was where the captain's housing was located. She stepped to the end of the sidewalk to get a better look. She turned to walk a few steps and saw a lovely house with grass, trees and a garden. It was already growing and heavy with a harvest of fresh vegetables. She was quite surprised and turned to tell the others.

She found the group right behind her. They had followed, waiting for her to give the approval that Fort Worth was acceptable and that they would be staying after all.